THE
RED
BANDANNA

David John Smith

ORCA BOOK PUBLISHERS

Canadian Cataloguing in Publication Data
Smith, David John, 1947 –
The red bandanna

ISBN 1-55143-138-6

1. Coyotes—Juvenile fiction. 2. Cariboo Region (B.C.) — Juvenile fiction. I. Title.
PS8587.M52445R42 1999   jC813'.54   C99-910037-8   PZ7.S64466Re 1999

Library of Congress Catalog Card Number: 98-83009

Canada
Orca Book Publishers gratefully acknowledges the support of our publishing programs provided by the following agencies: the Department of Canadian Heritage, The Canada Council for the Arts, and the British Columbia Arts Council.

Cover design by Christine Toller
Cover and interior illustrations by Ljuba Levstek
Printed and bound in Canada

IN CANADA:
Orca Book Publishers
PO Box 5626, Station B
Victoria, BC Canada
V8R 6S4

IN THE UNITED STATES:
Orca Book Publishers
PO Box 468
Custer, WA USA
98240-0468

01 00 99 5 4 3 2 1

*This book is dedicated to
Jessica and Jaime Skinner*

Thank you to those who read early drafts of the manuscript and offered their comments. Many improvements were made by this process. Colleen O'Neil and her son Jake, Jessica and Jaime Skinner, Cathryn Wellner, Richard Wright, and Karen Zilke.

Others helped in different ways — Michael Mulrooney, Debbie McKechnie, Steve Nelson, Bob Tyrrell. Thank you.

And thank you to Judy Hayes, my best friend for twenty-eight years, who did the above and so much more, all with a love supreme.

Table of Contents

Chapter 1
The Scrawny Coyote

Jake and Willy had ridden into Cougar Creek for ice cream cones and were on their way home. With barely a kilometre to go, Willy shouted, "Race you to your laneway?"

Jake pumped harder to catch up. When their front tires were even, he yelled, "Loser sucks rocks!"

"Yeah. Right," Willy called back.

"Go, go, go!" Jake shouted, and the race was on.

Jake Grant pulled half a bike length ahead off the start. He was taller than average for eleven, and was slim and strong. Willy Priedens was his neighbour and best buddy. She was a few months older, a little bit bigger and a little bit stronger than Jake.

Jake kept an eye on Willy's front tire, and whenever she started to gain on him, he poured more on. He loved the wind in his face. It was spring, and the sun was shining, and going fast made it all better. Now they were going downhill, and suddenly Willy's front tire was even with Jake's handlebars. She was gaining. The bikes were exactly the same, so no advantage there. But while the speed downhill was a bit scary to Jake, it only made Willy want more. She tucked, and immediately gained again, up to Jake's front axle now. They both stopped pedalling, letting their momentum and the hill home do the rest. Then Willy tucked even lower and, to Jake's amazement, she laid out flat. Her feet straight out behind, her nose almost touching the handlebars, she sped ahead screaming, "Suckerrrr!"

"Whoa," Jake yelled. He tucked, too, but he wouldn't lie down on the seat with his legs out behind.

Willy screamed past the laneway, then straightened up and hauled on her brakes. She skidded sideways, sliding her left foot along the road so she wouldn't fall, and finally came to a stop in a cloud of dust. Jake was waiting for her fifty metres back up the hill where the road met his lane. He was laughing as he watched Willy shift into low, then pedal back up.

A black pickup sped up to them, blaring the horn, then slammed on the brakes and skidded to a stop. The driver was Griff Webster, Jake's neighbour. Jake had never met the man, but he'd heard a lot, and none of it good. But Griff had known Willy all her life. He backed up almost to the laneway and waited for her. The big man smiled as he watched Willy panting toward them.

"What'd you do, miss the turn?" Griff said.

"Naw, I couldn't slow down till I got here. I mean, I had to win the race."

"Least I'd expect of you, Willy. How's the old man?"

"He's fine. Working hard as usual."

"Least I'd expect of him, too. He's a good one, your pa. So who's this young fella?"

Willy said, "This is Jake, our new neighbour. This is Griff Webster."

Griff reached out of his truck and shook hands with Jake.

"How do you do, sir," Jake said.

"Got a grandson about your age. How old anyway?"

"Eleven," Jake replied.

"Eleven," Griff repeated. "My boy's ten."

He stared intently at Jake, and something that

Jake didn't really understand passed between them. Then all of a sudden Griff looked surprised, like something had snuck up on him. He drove away fast.

Jake and Willy looked at each other and Willy shook her head. "Old Griff," she said. "His wife died a while ago. Pop says he's been weird ever since."

"Yeah, never met him before, but I heard about him. You're crazy, you know, lying out flat like that."

"Thanks," Willy beamed.

Wilhemena Priedens was lithe and tall, four centimetres taller than her best friend Jake. Her fair skin contrasted with her coal-black hair, but most remarkable were her big round eyes, set deep in an oval face. Her face was startlingly feminine, exquisitely delicate. The more Willy realized this, the more determined she was to show the world that she could work, play and, yes, even fight, alongside any boy. She had lived in the Cariboo all her life, the youngest and only girl in a family with five kids. Her nearest brother, Shamus, was eight years older. They lived on a big cattle ranch a few kilometres farther down on the Cougar Creek Road. She hated the name Wilhemena and insisted that everyone call her Willy, and everyone except her mother did. Willy lived the ranch life with her four brothers—plenty of good, satisfying work. She loved it.

While Jake was shorter than Willy, he was stockier, more muscled in a lumbering sort of way. Jake looked strong and athletic, and he was both of these things. He also looked like he would be "good in the corners," as his father, a hockey fan, said it. But rough stuff held no interest for Jake. He was a gentle soul. His eyes were an intense blue and always seemed to have a far-away look about them. "Yes, I'm here," they seemed to say, "and I'm listening. But there is also this other part of me that's somewhere else." Jake Grant was a contemplator.

While Willy was gung-ho and practically pure action, Jake liked to think things over first. He was a steady, serious kid raised in the city. He had moved to the Cariboo with his little sister, Elsa, and his mom and dad less than a year earlier. Six-year-old Elsa was not as happy with their move to the Cariboo as Jake was. There weren't any kids her age amongst their neighbours, so she missed her friends. She liked her new school, though, and she was gradually becoming comfortable with the quiet country way of things.

The ride down their laneway to the house was downhill, so they coasted, giving their legs a rest.

When they braked to a stop outside the kitchen window, Willy said, "Wasn't your mom baking cookies when we left?"

"Good old Will," Jake was thinking. He himself had forgotten this, even though his mom spent almost every Saturday morning baking cookies. "Let's go get some."

Just then Jake's mom came out the door carrying two glasses of milk. Cradled between her arm and her chest was a tin of cookies.

"Hey, Mrs. G., my pal!"

"I thought you two might have worked up yet another appetite."

"Appetite?" Willy grinned. "Why, I'm so hungry I could eat the — "

"Willy Priedens, I do not want to hear how hungry you are. If you finish what you were going to say, you will not eat a single one of my cookies."

"My lips are sealed," Willy teased, reaching for a handful of still warm peanut butter cookies.

Jake knew what Willy didn't say, and he laughed. "You've got more nerve than I have," he said.

They ate a handful of cookies each plus a few more and washed them down with milk, then set to work on their bikes. Jake carried tools, a pump and a patch kit on every trip, while Willy no longer had the pump that came with her bike. She had used it to blow up a tire on their wheelbarrow and had forgotten to put it back. Willy's approach to bike fixing was equally casual — fiddle a bit and then try it, and if that doesn't work then fiddle some more. Jake was the opposite. He got a book from the library on multi-speed bikes and had registered for a repair course that would start as soon as school finished in a few weeks. Jake sometimes wished he could be more like Willy, but being that casual just wasn't right for him. Willy, of course, never wished she was like anyone else. She was perfectly content to be herself.

Jake's bike wouldn't shift into the lowest gear, while Willy's brakes were soft. Willy's was easy to fix, more tension on the cables and change the pads. Jake did this, and while Willy went for a spin to try it out, he looked up gear changing in his book. It was a long section. He settled in with the three cookies he still had left and tried to make sense of it all.

Willy skidded to a stop in front of him. "Can I have one?"

Jake tossed her a cookie. "No wonder your brakes wear out."

"Your dad in the barn?" Willy asked.

"I think so."

"I'm going to say hi."

Willy's and Jake's dads were friends, too. Jake's dad, Mr. G., Willy called him, was a writer first. He had several books in print, but there was never any money until his mother willed him their old house in Vancouver. Suddenly he could afford that ranch he had always dreamed of. So Mr. G. was a Cariboo rancher, but he was a gentleman rancher still; even his eleven-year-old neighbour Willy taught him something new about ranching pretty much every time they got together.

It turned out that Mr. G. wasn't in the barn, so Willy checked out the pigs and then ambled back to the yard where Jake still had his nose in the bike book.

"Not there," Willy said. "Must be out in the field somewheres."

Jake looked around. "Guess so. The Massey's gone."

"Got a sow going to drop, eh?"

"Yeah?"

"Any day now, I figure."

"Jeez, I don't think Dad knows. I think he thinks maybe a couple of weeks yet."

"Pop can tell for sure. I'll ask him to stop by."

"Okay."

"What the — " Willy said.

"What?"

"Coyote. Just come out of the woodshed!"

"No way."

"No guff. There he is."

The coyote dashed out of the woodshed, leaped over the fence and sat down in the tall grass around an old tractor about fifty metres into the field. He was watching them.

"He sure isn't scared of us," Willy said.

"They usually scared of people?"

"Not so much scared, they just usually stay away."

Jake had never seen a coyote this close before. He had sure heard them, though. All winter he had been listening to their lonely, eerie call. He climbed the fence and started slowly toward him.

"What are you doing?" Willy asked.

"I just want to talk to him."

"Talk to him! Nobody talks to coyotes."

Not wanting to challenge the wary animal, Jake was careful not to make eye contact as he walked slowly into the field.

"What the — "

"Shh," Jake interrupted Willy, "and stay there."

Chapter 2:
Jake Felt Dumb, Dumb, Dumb

The coyote cocked his head to one side. His slender, intelligent face looked very curious.

Jake took a bite out of one of his last two cookies and chewed.

This, you could see on the coyote's face, was interesting.

Then Jake broke off a piece of cookie and tossed it onto the ground about halfway between them.

Very interesting. The coyote stood, looked all around, sniffed in the direction of the cookie, then casually moved a metre or so closer. He sat down again.

Jake appeared to take another bite.

The coyote sniffed and sniffed. Very, very interesting.

Jake stood up, walked off several steps and then stopped, still facing away from the coyote.

The coyote cocked his head again, again that intense curiosity. He shifted closer. Sniff, sniff and then more sniffing, and finally he couldn't hold back any longer. He scurried forward and quickly took the cookie bit into his mouth and then lay down in the grass, his eyes fixed on Jake, the cookie bit held lightly between his teeth.

Jake turned a bit toward the coyote. The animal's tail wagged once.

He thought that the coyote might be waiting for permission to eat. "Go right ahead," he said.

The coyote chewed and chewed and chewed and finally swallowed.

Then, speaking in a soft, low voice: "All right, then," Jake said. "I understand what you want. Thinking about food, aren't you? I know what that's all about, I like food myself." And then he stopped talking and looked here and there into the sheep pasture.

The coyote cocked his head one way and then the other and then back again.

Jake turned toward him now and extended his hand, the last bit of peanut butter cookie held at the tip of his fingers. "Here you are then, you mooch."

In a flash the cookie was gone. He wasn't afraid, he was just being careful.

Jake laughed, then walked smartly back to the fence, jumped it and headed back to his bike. Willy was staring at him.

"What's the matter with you?"

"Now you're crazy," Willy said.

"He's not very wild, is he?"

"Wild or not, if my Uncle Mark was here he'd take care of him."

"No way!"

"Darn right. Coyotes," she pronounced it ki-oat-eez, "are a menace. 'Pesky varmints,' Uncle Mark says. He shoots them whenever he can."

"Your dad too?"

"Naw, Dad wouldn't shoot hardly anything."

This one hadn't gone very far, just a few metres away, where he lay down to savour his cookie.

"Sure a scrawny lookin' thing."

"I guess, eh."

"Tame though, I bet, eh?"

"Seems like it," Jake replied.

"Where'd you learn that, talkin' to ki-oat-eez?"

"No place."

"I wonder what he was doin' in the woodshed."

"Yeah, I wonder."

Just then they heard a "yip yip." They turned to see the scrawny coyote a few feet from the fence, sitting as pretty as a show dog.

"What now?" Willy said.

Jake dropped to one knee. "Kneel down," he ordered. Willy obeyed without thinking.

Jake lowered his voice, and without looking directly into the coyote's eyes, he called, "Here boy, come on."

The coyote moved toward him, but stopped about halfway and sat.

Jake called again, "Come on now, nobody's going to hurt you."

The coyote came closer and stopped again. He lifted his head, looked Jake square in the eye, then ran across the field toward the bush.

"Wow!"

They watched as the coyote bounded the length of the field and disappeared into the sunlight.

"Incredible! I can't wait to tell Pop." Willy was the only kid Jake had ever met who called her dad Pop. "I gotta go anyway, help load cattle. I'll ask Pop to stop by and check on that sow."

"Okay, see ya."

"See ya."

Jake watched his best friend ride hard up to

the top of the laneway, then he walked to the woodshed to look it over. It had a sloping roof — about ten feet high at the open end so you could swing an axe — and a back, but no front or sides. The logs for their wood-burning furnace were stacked in rows about two metres tall and four long, and the rows were staggered so air could circulate around them. In the back corner there was something of a nest with sticks, leaves and a lot of fur where the coyote had been bedding down. This was home.

As he crouched to look closely at twigs with fur that seemed to have been wrapped around them, something made Jake turn around.

There was the coyote, sitting on his haunches, watching.

Jake stood up slowly, and this time he faced him directly. "Hi!"

The bushy tail wagged once.

"Don't go away. I'll be right back."

He moved sideways a few steps, then ran into the house. He was back moments later with half a peanut butter sandwich.

The coyote still sat on his haunches, but had turned toward the house. Jake walked away from the woodshed and sat down on the grass. He took a bite from his sandwich and slowly chewed, not paying any attention at all to the scrawny coyote.

The coyote watched Jake walk away, then, as he sat down, he cocked his head to the side and his slender, intelligent face again looked very curious.

Jake broke off a piece of sandwich and tossed it between them.

The coyote looked at it. He looked at Jake, then moved closer, and sat again.

Jake watched the sheep in the next field.

The coyote lay down. Then he too looked away. But he couldn't maintain his disinterest and soon was creeping toward that small piece of peanut butter sandwich. A metre away he stopped.

Jake stood up and walked back into the house. From the kitchen window he watched as the coyote crept ever closer to the piece of sandwich and sniffed and sniffed and then took it into his mouth. Strange, Jake thought as he watched, as the coyote chewed and chewed and swallowed it down. But the coyote was eating so slowly. "Must be because it's peanut butter." At last the coyote swallowed. Then Jake watched him leap the fence in a graceful arc and once again disappear across the field.

Next day, Sunday, the woodshed had no coyote in it all day. Monday morning, nothing, and nothing again when the bus dropped him off in the afternoon. Jake was sad. He went back to the spot where he'd eaten the cookie on Saturday and sat down. Still wearing his school clothes, he sat on his books so he wouldn't get grass stains on his pants. He looked in the same direction he had looked then, across the field and into the sheep pasture. He felt certain the coyote was nearby. He could feel him. He knew that it sounded silly to say that he could "feel" him nearby, but, silly or not, it was true. Jake counted sheep; there were forty-seven. He was sitting there, not thinking anything, watching birds slice through the clear blue sky, when he suddenly turned around and looked into the eyes of the coyote, sitting just a few metres behind him. His tail wagged one quick one.

Jake said, "Hi, Shadow. Glad to see you." The tail wagged a quick one again, and the ears dipped down, then came back up.

Jake had more peanut butter cookies in his shirt pocket. He broke one in two, popped one part into his mouth and tossed the other to Shadow.

Just then Mrs. G. opened the door of the house and stepped outside.

"Shadow," she called. "Come here."

The scrawny coyote ran to her, and she gave him a dog biscuit. He held the biscuit in his mouth, moved away a few metres and dropped it, finished chewing the cookie, swallowed by stretching his neck up and forward, then picked up the biscuit, ran across the yard, jumped the fence and was off.

Jake said to his mom, "How did you know his name?"

"I made it up. Do you like it?"

"It's great. It's the same one I came up with." You hardly ever saw him, yet he was always around, so Shadow just made sense. But amazing, Jake thought, how they both came up with the same name.

"Before you come in, would you go to the woodshed and see if there's still milk in her bowl?"

Bowl? What bowl? He hadn't noticed a bowl there when he checked just a bit ago. But sure enough, there it was, close against the woodpile. It was still half full of dry dog food. A second bowl was empty.

"How long have you known?"

"I've been watching her from the upstairs window since she first showed herself on Saturday."

"She? You think Shadow's a girl?"

"Of course, Shadow's a girl."

He felt dumb. He hadn't even thought about the swollen teats or the sagging belly.

"She's been around. She's just careful about approaching us."

"You mean she's been here these last few days when I thought she was gone?" In the kitchen now, he poured himself a glass of milk.

"All the time."

"You could see her?"

"Sometimes. She's often in the tall grass by the old tractor. But she moves around depending on the wind. She'll keep herself downwind of the woodshed so she can smell what's going on there."

Jake's mom had been raised on a prairie farm. She had come west thinking she would stay for a year, work as a secretary, then go back to Saskatchewan and settle down and get married. But she hadn't planned on meeting Jake's dad. Although she never did go back to the prairies, she'd always wanted to get out of the city. She loved animals and she loved those star-filled, quiet nights.

"Isn't it weird that a coyote will sleep so close to people?"

"Shadow's pretty tame; she's been around people. You can tell. She's careful, but she's not at all afraid. Have you been feeding her?" his mother asked.

"A little bit."

"Me too. She seems awfully hungry."

"So can we keep her?"

"I suppose. But really that's up to Shadow. Besides, it wouldn't be very nice to kick her out. She's going to have those pups any day now."

Jake felt dumb, dumb, dumb.

He went back outside carrying the glass of milk, both pockets filled with cookies. He also had the bike book under his arm, and an ensolite, a foam mattress that his dad used to carry on backpacking trips.

Shadow was gone, but he—she was probably lying down in the tall grass by the old tractor, chewing on her biscuit and keeping an eye on things. He was worried a bit that Shadow might not come back, but then he thought, "She's used to people; she'll be back." Besides, coyotes are just about the smartest animal around, his mom said. Jake laid the ensolite out, then sat down in his now favourite spot, overlooking the sheep pasture with his back to the woodshed. He set down his glass of milk, and then the book, and carefully stacked all his cookies into a pile beside him.

Before getting into the book that was teaching him all about fixing bikes, he looked around at what was happening with the day. One of Jake's greatest pleasures since moving to the Cariboo was having, for the first time in his life, four distinct seasons. The winter just passed had been typical, about two feet of snow, and consistent cold, often around minus twenty-five. Their brief spring was divided into two periods, crud and bud. Crud was when the melting snow exposed all the droppings and dirt that had been frozen in the snow all winter. Then, soon after the snow was gone, they were into the "bud" part, which was happening now—green grass in the fields and the aspens along their laneway just coming into bud.

Jake looked around, smelled the delicious freshness of the air and felt excited, more so than ever before, at the triumphant coming of spring. He turned to the book that was teaching him all about bike fixing and opened it to the section on changing gears.

Chapter 3
That Leather Collar

Jake and his mother sat down to supper that night feeling the hidden thrill of a shared secret. As far as they knew, neither Mr. G. nor Elsa knew anything at all about Shadow.

But the truth was that Mr. G. first saw Shadow that very day. On his way to the barn in the morning he was walking by the woodshed and heard a whimper. "Whoa, wood doesn't whimper," he said to himself. He stopped. Another whimper. He looked in the corners behind the wood and discovered a coyote looking up at him with loving, beseeching and very hungry eyes. She wagged her tail. He didn't try to touch her, but he did figure out that she was a girl and also that she was pregnant. Her winter coat was thinning, with patches of fur falling off and gathering here and there on her nest. But something unusual was around her neck. Mr. G. held out his hand and she sniffed it, but when he went to pat her head she pulled away.

He went back inside. "Did you forget something?" Mrs. G. asked. She was making breakfast for Jake and Elsa.

"My jackknife," he said. "I sharpened it last night. I must have left it in my study." He didn't say anything about the coyote. Mr. G. waited in his study until she left the kitchen to make sure the kids were up. Then he went to the refrigerator and put together a meal of leftover roast beef, mashed potatoes and some of Elsa's cat Peebles' food. Then he poured a bowl of milk and took everything out to the shed and set it down for the scrawny coyote. She started to eat right away. Mr. G. then went on to do the chores, feeling pleased with himself.

He fed the pigs and chickens and the one sickly lamb, and then worked at building new pens and a new chute for loading and unloading cattle and pigs. After ripping out the old pens, he cleaned up and stacked the wood to be cut to furnace size before starting to build the new ones. He did good work. Whatever he built looked like it would last forever. He was proud of his carpentry skills. But

Mr. G. didn't have the animal skills of a good rancher. He counted on his wife for that.

And after being a writer for all of his adult life, he was in great shape for sitting at a desk all day, but when working physically, he needed to rest regularly. He thought he would check on their scrawny, uninvited guest. Mr. G. figured she would either be asleep or gone from the woodshed altogether. He was very surprised indeed when he looked behind the woodpile and she was still there, still eating the food he had brought her an hour ago.

While the milk bowl was empty, the food was barely half gone. "No wonder she's skinny," he said to himself as he watched her chew so slowly. She chewed and chewed and then swallowed with such difficulty, such effort, that Mr. G. felt sorry for her. He wanted to get a closer look at that thick ring of fur around her neck. Slowly he extended his hand, ever so slowly. She had taken another bite of food and was chewing and chewing. She stopped, sniffed Mr. G.'s fingers. He reached further to pat her. She growled. Not a timid "Maybe don't" type growl, but one that said, "Back off, buster."

He backed off and watched. She chewed and chewed and chewed some more and finally swallowed, again with that strained effort, stretching out her neck and tilting her head. Then, with about one third of the food still in her dish, she stood up, sniffed the empty milk bowl and turned toward Mr. G. as if to say, "Excuse me, please." He stepped aside and the scrawny coyote, a little bit less so now, trotted past him, leaped the fence and ran across the field and out of sight.

Mr. G. went back to work in the barn, built pens for a while, then decided to stop earlier than usual for lunch. On his way past the shed he checked behind the woodpile. Everything was the same as before. He went to the fence where he last saw her and scanned the field. Nothing broke the stillness of the windless spring day. Mr. G. was just about to leave for the house when he felt something cool and wet against his hand. He turned. She stood immediately behind him, almost grinning, he thought. She wagged her tail once, then deeked around him and leaped the fence. She ran to the old tractor and was quickly out of sight in the tall grass surrounding it. Mr. G. looked, but he couldn't see her. He headed for the house and the hot lunch that would soon be ready.

All day in school Jake couldn't concentrate. It was getting close to the end of the year, so he was trying to pay closer attention, to make exams go easier, but all he could think about was getting home and seeing Shadow.

Shortly after they arrived home from school, Elsa trundled into their kitchen and saw her brother sitting at the table reading his bike book and having a snack. She didn't want to talk. She wished she were invisible so that she could pass without being seen. She was very quiet. She told Jake she was not feeling well and was going upstairs to lie down.

"Fine, take a pill, Sis. You'll feel better in the morning."

But she didn't lie down. She waited until Jake had left the kitchen, going up to his room to do the bit of homework that he had. House rule, homework had to be done right after snack. It was a bit of a pain, but at least he got it over with.

Both Mr. and Mrs. G. were out in the barn looking after that pregnant sow. Willy's dad had dropped by earlier and sure enough, she was ready to have piglets any time. Elsa sneaked downstairs. She wasn't sure when her parents were coming back, so she had to be ready to be doing something normal, like sitting at the kitchen table eating a bowl of cereal, her favourite snack. She poured a big bowl of Cheerios and cut a banana onto them and spread sugar all over. Then, climbing onto a chair and peeking out the window to be sure that no one was coming, she carried the bowl out to the shed.

Elsa set the bowl down behind the woodpile. The other bowls were empty except for some roast beef in one, which she barely noticed and didn't think about. Then she walked to the fence and called, "You can come out now," and ran back into the kitchen, climbed onto the counter and watched through the window. Shortly, the coyote appeared. She bounded over the fence and ducked into the shed out of sight. Elsa watched until she got tired of watching, then went into the living room to practise piano. She loved her new teacher, an elderly woman who lived nearby in a log house, and Elsa was determined to do a good job of the week's lesson.

At the supper hour, Mr. and Mrs. G. came in for dinner. It would be leftovers because they had been busy with the sow, but the kids loved leftovers anyway. At the dinner table Elsa didn't say anything about the coyote exactly, but she did ask if they could get a dog.

There was a long silence and finally Mr. G. said, "Well, that's something we'll have to think about. Having a dog carries a great deal of responsibility, you know. If we were to get one, you and Jake would have to promise to feed him every day — "

"Her," Elsa said.

"What?"

"I want a girl dog."

"Alright then, you will have to feed her every day and make sure she gets exercise."

Jake and Elsa said that they would and that they would bath her and pet her and take her for walks.

Jake and his mom looked at each other, and although Mrs. G.'s face was blank, Jake couldn't help but grin. Elsa knew too; that was obvious. And he was pretty sure that his father knew. And of course Jake knew that his mom knew and she knew that Jake knew. All that had to happen then was that they would say to each other that Shadow was already part of the family. But nobody seemed to want to come out with it. They all looked at each other and smiled. Elsa and Jake almost burst from holding it in. Finally Mr. G. said, "I'm not very hungry tonight. What do you think, Jean, should we put the rest of this back in the fridge or do you have another use for it?"

"I think I could find a good use to put it to. I
noticed a bag of dog food in the back of the truck.
What if I mix it up with some of that and leave it
in a dish in the woodshed and see what happens?"

Elsa and Jake looked at each other and right
away they smiled, and Mr. and Mrs. G. did too,
so everybody knew. There was nothing left to do
but celebrate. The kids jumped up from the table,
both talking at once: "I want to feed her."

"Can I feed her? I fed her before. She's my
dog, really, I saw her first." And then Mr. G. said,
"Enough already, we'll all feed her."

Mrs. G. went out to the truck and came back
with a bag of dog food and a stainless steel dish.
Pouring dry bits into the bowl, she said that they
had to give Shadow just good dog food with a little
bit of leftovers because people food wasn't good for
dogs. This didn't seem right to Jake and Elsa because Shadow sure liked Cheerios and peanut butter
cookies. Mrs. G. filled the stainless-steel bowl with
food and another one with milk. "Dogs love milk,"
she said, and they all went out to the shed.

Shadow was there, but not asleep. She had finished eating her Cheerios with milk and banana
and sugar and had finished the food Mr. G. had
brought her, and was lying down looking happy,

with empty food dishes all around. She knew they were doing something special. They stood around her, Mr. and Mrs. G. looking over the woodpile and the two kids looking around the end of it. Elsa and Jake set the bowls down beside her. She looked at them but didn't move. "Go on," Elsa said, "you're part of the family now. We're going to feed you every day." But Shadow wouldn't budge. She looked from one to the other and then back again. And then suddenly she looked nervous.

Jake knelt down. Shadow came and sat in front of him and he petted her for the first time. She let him pet her and pet her. The rest of the family stepped back because they realized that something special was happening. He hugged her. Then he said, "This isn't right," feeling the thick ring of fur around her neck. He felt some more. There was something underneath all that fur. It was a leather collar. It was a thick leather collar, and there was skin and fur grown up around it. He thought for a moment, remembering how she chewed and chewed and chewed and how she stretched her neck out when she swallowed, and he knew what had to be done.

"Dad," he said, "could I borrow your jack-knife?"

His father opened the knife he had just sharpened the day before and passed it to Jake handle first. Jake cut carefully through the collar. Taking it off was difficult because so much fur had grown around it. But Shadow sat perfectly still. She trusted Jake. She may not have understood what was happening, but she trusted this new person in her life.

When Jake finally got the collar off and dropped it on the ground, Shadow sniffed it thoroughly. Then she nudged Jake's hand and dodged her way out of the shed and quick as a flash leaped over the fence and ran across the field, past the old tractor in the island of tall grass, and fast, fast toward the bush.

The Grant family was stunned.

They went back inside.

Nobody wanted dessert. Mrs. G. cleared the table and Mr. G. and Jake did the dishes. Then Elsa and Jake watched out the window for Shadow. They were sad. When Mr. and Mrs. G. went back to the barn, Jake and Elsa walked around looking for her. After dark they stayed in the house, but looked and called out the windows. At bedtime Jake went out to the shed and checked, and the milk and the dog food were still there and Shadow was still gone. Nobody understood. Elsa didn't get a story read to her that night. Both her mom and her dad were still out in the barn, but she didn't feel like having one anyway. She fell asleep and dreamed of riding across the fields on Shadow's back.

Jake couldn't sleep. He moved his pillow to the foot of his bed and lay there looking out the window. He thought he had done Shadow a kindness by cutting off that heavy collar. A collar that some unthinking person must have put on when she was a puppy, and then she must have got away. But maybe now that she was free to eat like a normal coyote she would never come back. Maybe all she needed people for was to feed her because she couldn't chew right.

His mother had said that coyotes mated for life and were very smart. Jake wondered if Shadow had a mate. He wondered if maybe the mate hadn't had close contact with people like Shadow, so was staying away. He wondered if maybe the two of them weren't out hunting right now and didn't need the food they had left in the shed. He wondered if Shadow, being almost wild, didn't like the food they gave her.

Jake still had his clothes on. The window looked out over their backyard, and then across the field where the old tractor was. He got up and closed his bedroom door, because the hall light was making it hard to see outside. Then he lay back down and peered into the darkness. He was trying to see into the field. At first he couldn't see very well, but he knew that as time passed his eyes would adapt and he would be able to see much better. Then he heard two shots. Quick, one right after the other. He peered into the black, trying to will Shadow back to the safety of their shed, but he couldn't see a thing. Then he heard another. "Kill shot," Jake said aloud.

Chapter 4
Very, Very Pregnant

Jake slept lightly, as he always did when he was worried. He was still at the foot of his bed, but he had pajamas on and was covered with blankets. His mom must have come in during the night, but he didn't remember this. He looked out at the day. Spring was in full bloom. The apple trees in the orchard were budding up; the sheep seemed to be moving with a new lightness, and the pasture was a deep, rich green. Jake studied their backyard, searching for some sign that Shadow had come back. Nothing that he could see. He got out of bed, dressed quickly and ran downstairs. Those three shots just before he fell asleep were still ringing in his ears.

"Where are you going?" his mom said.

"I have to see if Shadow's back."

In peejays and bare feet, Jake ran to the wood-shed and peered into the back corner. No Shadow and nothing eaten. His heart sank. He walked slowly back inside, not even noticing that it was cold again.

Jake and Elsa wanted to stay home and look for Shadow, but their mom and dad said no way. All day in school they were sad and thought of little else. When they got off the bus that afternoon, they rushed to the shed: still no Shadow; still nothing eaten. Jake dragged himself into the house and for the first time in his life he didn't have a snack. Elsa wasn't hungry either, and she started to cry. Mrs. G. held her head in her lap and stroked her hair, while Jake looked out the window. He felt that he was being smothered by a heavy, black cloud that had been surrounding him ever since hearing those shots. He knew that Griff Webster shot coyotes, wolves and wild dogs, any animal that prowled near the livestock, and he wondered if maybe Shadow hadn't been Griff's latest victim. Maybe cutting off that collar hadn't been such a good thing after all. Then, just as he turned to say something to his mom, he heard a yip. He knew who it was. They all knew. If ever a sound rang with happiness, it was when Shadow yipped. Jake heard it and so did Mrs. G. and so did Elsa.

They ran out to the woodshed, but Shadow wasn't there. They ran to the bushes beside the house, to the bushes behind the house. Not there either. They looked everywhere they could think of, and then went back inside, where Elsa helped Jake watch. Mrs. G. made tea. She always made tea when she got excited.

Shortly they heard two more yips, each one from a different place. Shadow was running. When she ran by and saw Jake in a window, she yipped.

"I just saw her," he shouted, "and she yipped when she saw me!"

Shadow ran around the house. Whenever she passed a window with someone in it she yipped. Was she going crazy? Shadow ran past the living room window where Jake and his mom were. She yipped. Then she flashed past the kitchen window where Elsa was and she yipped again. Shadow wasn't crazy; she was having fun.

They all ran outside. Shadow was smiling and happy, but she pulled away when Mrs. G. and Elsa reached out to her. Jake stood back and then watched with pride as Shadow walked around them and sat smartly in front of him. She wagged her tail and licked his hand. Jake petted her and scratched behind her ears. He didn't say anything, but Shadow awakened something inside him that he had never before known.

Then suddenly Shadow ran into the wood-shed. They all hurried after her. Her food and milk were there, and she looked to each of them as though asking if it was okay if she ate it. They smiled and Elsa said, "Come on, Shadow, we're your family now." Shadow wagged her tail and ate in her awkward way, but much less so than before.

"She sure is skinny," Mrs. G. said. "If she's going to have pups, we'd better fatten her up."

"Mom," Jake said, "did you hear the shots last night after we went to bed?"

"Yes, were you worried?"

"A little bit," he fibbed.

From then on the Grants fed Shadow every morning and every evening. She was always out of sight at meal times, but shortly after Jake set the bowls of dog food and milk down in her corner of the woodshed, she would suddenly appear as though from nowhere and eat like she was half starved, as though she knew she had a lot to make up for. In just a few days she was chewing normally. No more stretching her neck out and swallowing slowly. Mrs. G. was worried that by

the time the pups were born Shadow might not
be strong enough, so she gave her lots of dry dog
food plus leftovers plus all the milk she could
drink. And Shadow could drink huge amounts.

After breakfast she would stroll away from the
shed and disappear, usually into the tall grass that
surrounded the old tractor, but she moved whenever the wind changed. Sometimes she slept, but
often she spent her time watching, keeping an eye
on the shed and looking out for things. She always seemed to Jake to be waiting for someone,
her mate maybe. Mrs. G. said if he did come,
Shadow would probably leave them forever.

Nighttime was different. Every evening
around dark Shadow trotted across the field and
disappeared into the trees. She was hunting, Mrs.
G. said. Coyotes always hunt at night and in the
daytime they hang around home and sleep and
keep an eye on things. Usually. But Shadow was
fed twice a day; she no longer had to hunt. Maybe
she was looking for her mate. Maybe she hunted
anyway, because that was the way things were with
coyotes. With Shadow it was impossible to tell
because nobody knew how much of her life had
been spent with people. Within a couple of weeks
of this easy living, Shadow was looking much
healthier and very, very pregnant. With only two

weeks left until the end of the school year, it was looking like the pups would be born right in the middle of exams. This worried Jake a little bit. But he forced himself to concentrate; he made sure his schoolwork was done right so he would be free to pay attention to Shadow. Jake liked doing well in school, but suddenly Shadow was the most important thing in his life. He wanted to be with her all the time.

As she got fatter, she went to the woods less and less. Soon Shadow was staying in the shed all night, coming out only for a walk during daylight. Mrs. G. thought she looked painfully pregnant. This was surely her first litter, and it was surely a big one, six or eight pups, maybe more.

The first time Mrs. G. sat with Shadow, Shadow nudged her hand and asked for a pet. She was thrilled. It was an honour, she said, to be accepted by Shadow.

She had the vet come by to check on her, but Shadow didn't like the vet and wouldn't let him touch her.

Jake was first in Shadow's heart, but as the birthing time got closer, she spent more and more time with Mrs. G, as though Shadow knew that she was the only one who really understood about having babies. Jake didn't want to leave Shadow alone, though. Soon his mom and dad gave up trying to keep him to his usual routine.

Jake was spending so much time with Shadow that he wasn't getting enough sleep, so he brought a foamy into the woodshed and slept there in his sleeping bag. As soon as they were together, they each fell asleep. As soon as one of them went away, the other woke up, as if they were tied to each other with invisible strings. If Jake went inside the house to go to the bathroom, Shadow waddled to the back door and waited until he came out. If he went to the barn to do his chores, Shadow followed right behind him. She would never go into the barn, though, not where there were other animals. She knew where she wasn't wanted.

Soon Shadow got so big she could barely get around. Jake took her for waddles. They waddled back to the woods behind the house, and Shadow would stop in her favourite spot, a place where the grass was smooth and soft, and the sun shone through the trees, and there was a log for Jake to sit on. She would lie down and Jake would pet her, and every once in a while she would lick his hand. Once they sat this way for over two hours. "The most peaceful spot on earth," Jake called it.

Soon Shadow went out waddling less and less.

She was so fat with puppies that every movement seemed to require a huge effort. Jake was worried. It seemed that if Shadow got any bigger she would burst. Jake would get her outside the shed, but after a short waddle Shadow would sit down, and as soon as Jake stopped, she would start back. Near the birthing time she would barely go outside the shed at all, just enough to pee and do her business, then back to lie down. She was still eating a lot, though, and drinking milk almost constantly. Jake was amazed at how much she could eat, and amazed as well to watch Shadow's belly wiggle. It seemed to him that there were twenty-eight puppies inside, all playing soccer at the same time, her belly wiggled so much.

Chapter 5
Puppies

It was just before eleven o'clock on Friday night. In his peejays and bare feet, Jake slipped quietly into the kitchen from the backyard, switched off the outside light, then closed the kitchen door and hurried back to the shed. He shone his flashlight in the direction of Shadow, who was lying in the corner and looking for all the world as though she was about to die from the sheer exhaustion of breathing. Careful not to shine the light directly into her face, Jake peered at her. Nothing was any different. Still the impossibly fat belly that never stopped bulging and wiggling, and still the impossibly swollen teats that looked ready to burst.

He dipped his finger into the milk dish and

held it at Shadow's nose. Her eyes were open, but they didn't appear to see. Jake touched a drop of milk to her nose, and with a heroic effort, she licked it off, thereby getting the tiniest amount of her absolutely favourite food. He dipped again, and tried again, but this time Shadow ignored it. She was too tired to lick. Jake wiped his fingers on his peejay bottoms, then wriggled into the sleeping bag on top of the foamy that was just half a metre from Shadow.

Like Shadow, he couldn't sleep, but now, with the yard light out, at least he could feast his eyes on the stars, a million of them, a zillion of them, more than he ever saw from his old house in Vancouver. More, probably, than anywhere else on earth. Although it had taken almost a year, Jake Grant decided, as he lay there too tired or too excited to sleep, that he very much liked living in the Cariboo.

This was his third night sleeping out. He had a good sleeping bag and a double layer of ensolite, and, of course, his own foamy that he took camping. And Jake had a flashlight, and rubber boots, and his winter coat, in case he needed it. His mom had filled a thermos with hot chocolate, and he had a sandwich and cookies for a bedtime snack. Everything.

Without leaving his sleeping bag, he could dip his finger into the milk and hold it for Shadow to lick. For three nights he had been doing this, sometimes for over an hour at a stretch. Jake would have done it for thirty hours if Shadow had wanted him to. But this last hour or so all she could manage was one or two licks before slipping back into exhaustion.

Over the last two nights Shadow had been sleeping, but not this night, and so far Jake couldn't fall asleep either. That's why he wanted the light off. If he couldn't sleep and if Shadow didn't need feeding, then he might as well stare at the stars.

The shed roof was high and slanted so a person could cut wood under it and keep out of the weather. Jake was lying on the ground just under the outside edge of the roof. To his right were the rows of stacked firewood and the roof and the back of the shed, slats with the light of the sky shining through in milky slivers, while to his left the half-dome of the sky was blue-black and brilliant.

Jake, though determined to be with Shadow regardless, had expected to be afraid of sleeping outside on his own. And he *had* been afraid, when he thought about it that first night, but not at all

since then. This night, with the yard light out for the first time, he wondered what it was he'd been afraid of.

As he lay there staring up at the night sky, he had a strange feeling. For the first time in his life, he felt BIG! He didn't feel that he was eleven years old or even fifteen years old or twenty. It was a weird sensation; he just felt BIG. He didn't try to analyze the feeling, although he did remind himself that this was another one of those things he wouldn't tell Willy or anyone else. The stars and the sky, both very big, were a part of this feeling, but so was Shadow, and so was he, lying there excited and unafraid. Jake thought about this a lot, but couldn't figure it out in any clear way. The closest he could come was to say that this BIG feeling was something very special, like the special feeling he had for Shadow, and that he thought Shadow had for him.

First light graced the eastern sky. Jake woke with a start. He shone his flashlight in Shadow's direction, but off to the side so he didn't shine the brightest of the light right into her face. Her eyes were wide open. Jake was angry with himself for falling asleep. Shadow was awake; he shouldn't have been sleeping at all. He dunked his finger into the milk and held it to Shadow's nose. He felt the barest hint of her warm, shallow breath. But she wouldn't or couldn't lick.

Jake wriggled out of his sleeping bag and ran across the yard, through the back-porch door and then upstairs to his parents' room.

"Mom, you gotta come right away. Shadow's dying; I fell asleep and she's hardly breathing at all. Please, right now, please."

His mother's feet touched the floor just as he said his last please. "Put two cups of milk in a saucepan on the stove. In the bottom cupboard to the right of the sink there's a plastic baby bottle. Wash it with really hot water. I'll be there as soon as I get dressed."

Jake ran back to the kitchen and did exactly as he was told. When his mom came down, she was dressed in warm clothes and looked like she expected to be outside for quite a while. Jake had washed out the bottle, and the milk was on high.

"It doesn't have to be boiling," she said, "just warm. And you should have more on. Where's your coat?"

"In the shed."

"Go put it on. Socks and boots, too."

Jake ran back to the woodshed. Shadow was the same, barely breathing, with no reactions to anything he did, not to milk on the fingers, not to being petted. All he could think to do was to pet her, stroking her head and her side. Jake felt scared. Scared enough to cry, but that was dumb. He forced himself to think, to think positively. He thought images of Shadow up and frisky and all these puppies playing around her.

He heard the back door and shortly his mother hurried out of the darkness and into the soft light of the kerosene lantern Jake had just lit. He stood back. He knew that his mom had a way with animals. He hoped she could do something now.

She talked to Shadow first and then rubbed her belly. When Shadow licked the dryness from her lips, Jake's mom rubbed more, massaging her belly gently. Shadow licked again, and then Jake's mom stuck the rubber tip of the baby bottle into her mouth and squeezed. Some of the warm milk ran off onto the ground, but Shadow licked it up, and she licked again and swallowed. Another squirt. Less of it ran off this time, and pretty soon Mrs. G. sent Jake back inside to heat up some more.

When he came back holding a saucepan of steaming milk, his mother was massaging Shadow's belly, the baby bottle was empty, and there were two hairless, eyeless, fat creatures sucking like mad on Shadow's teats. He almost dropped the milk.

"Holy smokes, it's happening."

"Get that into the bottle, and see if she'll take any more. I'm going to keep massaging her. It seems to be helping."

Jake did as he was told. Then he tilted the bottle into Shadow's mouth and watched the show. He was amazed. Their eyes were closed and they were pink and had no fur at all and they looked like slightly overgrown bald mice, but they knew right where to go for food. The next one popped out and Jake said, "We'd better start naming them quick or we're going to lose track. This one, he's the first one, isn't he, Mom?"

"That's right."

"How be ... let me think, now."

"How about Rick?" Mrs. G. said.

"Okay, Rick then. Now this guy."

"Girl."

"Okay, girl. How about — Ellen?" and he laughed because just as he said it she peed. Immediately another popped out. Mrs. G. called him Coop. Rather than going to a vacant teat, he pushed Ellen away and used hers, then, after drinking just a bit, he went after Ellen again. Coop was very small and he was more interested in fighting than he was in eating. "Figures," Mrs. G. said.

The fourth puppy was a girl. She was not at all

interested in fighting with Coop. She was skinny and ever so small, and Mrs. G. said, "Oh, doesn't she look prissy. We'll call her Nikki." Nikki seemed to hear her name and turned her head toward Mrs. G. She named the fifth one Steve, because he reminded her of her brother. Steve popped out and shuffled over to Mrs. G, ignoring the teat and his mother altogether. Mrs. G. directed him back and then had to open his mouth and put it around Shadow's teat before he got the idea and started to suck. Her brother always said that he would rather be a puppy of his sister's than a human being, she treated them so well.

The pups kept popping out as fast as Jake and Mrs. G. could come up with names. Shadow had stopped sucking the bottle, so Jake would squirt a bit of milk onto her tongue, wait for her to swallow and then squirt some more. He felt excited and at the same time calm, and he was very, very glad that his mom was there.

Then came Colleen. She was Mrs. G.'s best friend. Colleen was not big, not small, and she knew just where to go for food.

Number seven Mrs. G. called Tee Kay. All she said was that Tee Kay was an old friend of hers. She didn't give any explanations.

Number eight she named Auntie Jude. She was

small and pretty, like Auntie Jude herself. She couldn't find the last free teat, so Mrs. G. showed her where to go.

Mikey was next, and next to last, and he had to scramble his way to a teat, knocking Nikki out of the way with his nose. Nikki bumped into Steve; then he was without a place and he went after someone else. Pretty soon Mrs. G. couldn't tell who was who and it didn't matter anyway.

The last puppy born was the smallest of all. He popped out and didn't move, as if he had made it this far, it was up to somebody else now. Mrs. G. moved him against Shadow's belly, but he was not interested. First she called him Mel, but then she changed it to Number Ten. She knew that this was it. Shadow shifted her place and went to sleep. Jake sat back and stared in wonder. Number Ten didn't do anything at all. Finally Mrs. G. dipped her finger into the milk. Ten liked this, so Mrs. G. dipped again, and Ten licked again. Then she put him up to a teat, but Number Ten would have none of it. He wanted Mrs. G.'s finger. Jake wanted to try, so he dipped into the milk dish and Ten licked his finger too.

"You really think that's it?"

"I sure hope so. Ten pups is an awful lot. I don't think Shadow could take any more. I'm not even sure she can handle this."

"Number Ten is easy to tell. He's the littlest of all."

"And not at all interested in feeding from his mother."

Suddenly Shadow lifted her head and looked down at the mess of scrambling puppies. "Oh my God," she seemed to say.

Jake and his mom laughed.

Shadow licked Number Ten a few times, then her head dropped down to the ground again, and Jake stuck the bottle into her mouth and squeezed. With the other hand he dipped into the milk dish and held his finger for Number Ten to lick.

"Maybe you should go in and make tea. I'll do this for a while," Jake offered.

Mrs. G. watched him dipping into the milk and Number Ten feeding from his finger and she swelled with pride. Jake Grant, her son, and yes, making tea was a good idea too.

"Okay," she said.

Walking to the house, she realized that the sun was up. It was light out. It promised to be a true spring day, with some of the winter just passed and some of the summer to come.

Chapter 6
Good Neighbours

As Mrs. G. made sure each puppy got time on a teat and held the bottle for Shadow and dipped her finger for Number Ten, she found herself thinking about Jake. He seemed to grow up all in a surge with the birthing of the coyote pups. She gave him the choice of going to school that day or not. He was tired, yes, but it was Friday and close to the end of the year. Exams were coming soon. He wanted to ace them all so he wouldn't have to think about school all summer long. He didn't hesitate very long before deciding that he would go.

Mrs. G. was proud. She remembered what he was like as a child, and how he had worried her. When he was three, he had been playing by himself while she worked in the kitchen. She hadn't heard anything from him in a while. She went to his room and looked in the door. Jake was sitting in the centre of the floor staring up at the light, a bare bulb that hung from the ceiling. It was a dull day and their eastside Vancouver apartment was dark, so the light had to be on. He wasn't doing anything, just staring, eyes unblinking, with the most peaceful, most serene look on his face. Mrs. G. was afraid there was something wrong, because he didn't react to her. He seemed to be in some sort of trance. She went to him and put her hands on his shoulders to get him to stop looking at the light and to look at her, but still he seemed lost in a trance. Then his eyes turned to hers and suddenly she was filled with awe at this unusual creature who was her son. She felt a reverence for him. His sky-blue eyes looked so calm and peaceful and grown up, so mature. From then on it always made her feel peaceful to look into his eyes. There wasn't anything wrong with him at all. Whatever it was that made Jake different was something positive, something wonderful. She stopped worrying.

When the bus dropped Jake and Elsa at the end of their laneway later that day, Willy was there too. All three of them hurried down the lane to the shed.

"Hi, Mrs. G., what's for snack?"

She laughed. "I'm sure you could find some cookies somewhere."

"Wow! Are they ever little. They look like wet gophers."

Shadow was alert at the coming of three more people. Willy held back while Jake went to Shadow's head and stroked her. He took the bottle from his mom and squeezed some into Shadow's mouth. She relaxed and drank it down, a little more eager than she was that morning.

"She's getting better," Jake said.

"You think? I wasn't sure if she was any livelier or not."

"For sure. Are they all feeding from her?"

"They're all livelier except Number Ten. And he won't go near a teat. It's hard to get enough into him when the only way he'll feed is licking your finger."

"Okay if I try?" Willy said.

"Sure."

Willy held the tiniest of the ten pups and dipped her finger into the milk, then held it up for him to lick. Ten sucked and licked furiously, as usual. "Hey, I think she likes me." No sooner were the words out of her mouth than Ten pooped all over Willy's arm. "Ah, poo," Willy said.

"She's a he," Jake said, laughing.

"He, she, what the heck. You wouldn't poop on somebody you didn't like, would you?"

"Come on, Else, you try," Willy said.

Elsa took a bald and blind Number Ten and cradled him in the crook of her arm, then dipped her finger and held it like she did with her one doll. At six years old Elsa had already made it known that she would not be having a family. She would be having a career—as a dancer or a singer. She wasn't sure which. One doll was all that she needed. Just so that she was a "little bit" like other girls her age. Ten didn't care whether he was upside down or right side up, or who fed him, he just wanted to eat all the time.

"Is he ever fatter," Jake said.

"I've been feeding him all day. Willy, why don't you wash that off with the hose and then maybe you'll find a few cookies lying around inside. And, of course, a few glasses of milk, and I'd love a cup of tea. And Mr. G. would too, I bet. He's out in the barn with the sow."

Willy grinned at Jake's mom, then she left for the house, saying, "Right away, Mrs. G."

Elsa screamed. "He's wiggling! He's trying to get away!"

"Put him down then," Jake said.

She set Number Ten on the ground. Ten turned his head this way and that, seemingly trying to decide which way to go, then made a beeline for Jake and shuffled onto his shoe.

"Hey, little guy." He set the bottle down and picked up Number Ten. Ten had a full sniff of Jake's hand and then went to sleep.

"What do I do now?" Jake asked his mom.

She shrugged. "Take him for a walk. You should change out of your school clothes anyway."

Jake carried Number Ten inside. Willy was in the kitchen. She had filled a bowl with cookies, and the kettle was on to boil. There were three big glasses of milk on a tray.

"What's your mom take in her tea?"

"Milk and sugar."

"Milk and sugar it is, then. Who's that?"

"This," Jake said with pride, "is Number Ten. He wiggled away from Elsa and walked right over to me."

"Really," Willy said. "I wonder if he knows something."

Jake went upstairs to his room. He thought that was a funny thing for Willy to say. When he came back down, he asked.

"Hey, Will, why'd you say that?"

She was pouring boiling water from the kettle into the teapot. "Say what?"

"You said, 'I wonder if he knows something.'"

"I don't know. It's just, I mean, why'd he go to you? Must be a reason."

"Maybe, eh."

Jake curled Number Ten closer into his sweatshirted chest and went back out to the shed. As he walked along, he stroked Ten's forehead and tried to talk him into opening his eyes.

A short while later Willy came out carrying the tray with milk, cookies and a pot of tea and a cup for Mrs. G., and another for Mr. G.

Willy had felt comfortable with the Grants the first time she met them. It was the day they moved in. She and her dad had driven over to welcome them to the Cariboo. "City folk," her dad had said on their way back home. "I like that. A good neighbour is somebody you can help, and I get the feeling they're going to need plenty of that." On her way across the yard with the tray of goodies, Willy thought of her dad saying that and it made her smile.

"Hey," Mrs. G. said, "thank you."

Shadow woke up. She seemed to have a nose for cookies. "Look at that," Willy said. "She knows when snack time is."

Just then Hal Priedens and his wife, Marlene, drove their blue pickup into the yard. Mrs. G. watched them get out of the truck. She glanced at Willy, who was grinning broadly. Whatever was happening, this was planned. Marlene went into the house carrying a large steaming pot and, on top of this, a brown paper bag filled with something. Hal, Willy's dad, sauntered over to the shed.

"Something smells awful good," he said. "Must be prit near dinnertime."

Willy laughed. "Everybody else is eating. We may as well too."

"How you doin', Joan?"

"I'm fine, I think. How about you?"

"I'm good. I see you're keeping busy. First pigs and now these little gaffers. Holy smokes, look at them all."

"There's ten of the little suckers," Willy said.

"Well, I'll be go to hell. Ten pups, eight pigs. Life's good, eh? Well I better go check on them pigs now. Be back in just a bit."

"Here, Pop, take this to Mr. G. for me, please." She handed the teacup to her dad.

"Sure thing," Willy's dad said.

Willy's mom stepped outside and hollered, "Come and get it."

Willy added, "Deer stew and all the fresh buns you can eat. How's that sound, Mrs. G.?"

"You guys, honestly, I don't know what we did to deserve such wonderful neighbours. I guess we'd better hurry up and show our appreciation. What do you say, kids?"

"Yeah!" said Elsa.

"I guess so, eh," Willy laughed.

"Count me in," said Jake.

Shortly, Hal and Mr. G. came in from the barn. The stew was eaten and all of the fresh baked buns disappeared quickly. After dinner the Priedens drove home and Jake went back outside to feed Ten. He did lick a bit, but eating all day had made him tired and soon all he wanted to do was sleep. He curled into a ball in the midst of his brothers and sisters, who were clustered around Shadow's belly, and slept. Amazingly, so did all the others and Shadow, too.

Jake was tired, and for the first time in his life, he voluntarily went up to bed before his bedtime. But he found that he couldn't sleep. He moved his pillow to the foot of the bed and lay there thinking. It was dark. He had checked and re-checked and there were no animals near the shed, so Shadow and the puppies were safe. The only thing left was for him to fall asleep, and he couldn't. He felt privileged to have witnessed the pups being born. He was wideawake and felt excited, just like he would expect to feel at the start of a long, long journey.

Chapter 7
Neighbour with a Gun

Griff Webster took a can of beer from his refrigerator, lifted the top and pulled long. He lowered his large body onto a wooden chair at the kitchen table and kicked a telephone book and some newspapers off a nearby stool, resting his feet there instead. Griff had earlier bowed to Mrs. Janes, his occasional cleaning lady, removing his manure-covered boots in the mudroom. His wool socks were inside out.

He was ticked off. He had been at the co-op earlier that day and had run into Rafe and Mrs. Fairburn, who lived a few kilometres from him on the next road over. The missus had asked how he liked living next door to a coyote ranch. She had gone on to explain that his new neighbours, the Grants, city people, were raising coyote pups like they were a domestic animal and were letting them run free. Right next door, she'd said, surprised he hadn't heard.

Well, Griff Webster was not prepared to take lightly the raising of wild coyotes like they were household pets, the breeding of calf killers, on land next door to his ranch. He pulled again on the beer, and then once more, emptying the can, scrunched it in his big fist and tossed it in the general direction of the garbage can in the corner. Then he got a second beer from the fridge and sat back down. In his usual bedtime way, this one he would sip.

There were no gray areas in Griff Webster's world. If a thing wasn't good, then it was bad, if not white, then black, if not friend, then foe. A coyote was not his friend, therefore it was his enemy. A coyote was not good, therefore it was bad. And bad for Griff Webster was something to kill. Poison worked fine, but Griff preferred his rifle. It made a lot of noise, which he liked; he liked showing off his good shot and he liked the hunt itself. Outsmarting them.

He had not always been so harsh. Before his wife died three years ago, there had been joy in every step that he took, for he loved her more than life itself. He had children and grandchildren too. He spent his days raising cattle, the only thing he ever wanted to do.

Then a car accident changed all that. A head-on collision with a drunk driver. His wife was killed and so was his dog Trixie, a border collie-terrier cross who knew, Griff believed, his very thoughts, often before he himself was aware of them. The drunk walked away from the accident and also from jail after serving two months of a six-month sentence. He had come to Griff's house one Sunday afternoon after getting out of jail to say that he was sorry. Griff slammed the door in his face. Ever since the accident he had been either angry or on the verge of crying, one or the other. Griff didn't cry, though, never had, but he had been very, very angry.

For several months after his wife's death his three grown children, who lived down at the coast, visited regularly. He was never happy to see them, always negative, and did not appreciate the effort they made, so now they visited only at Christmas and again during the summer if they happened to be up country.

But visits or not, Griff no longer cared. He cared about them, of course, and about his seven grandchildren, but he couldn't seem to communicate this. The only emotion he could manage to show anyone was anger. His kids kept their kids away because they didn't want them to see their grandfather so totally negative. They hoped he would get over it. He was always a bit gruff, but there had been a twinkle in his eye when Mavis was around to remind him how good things could be. "Gruff Griff and Mavis," the kids used to joke.

And he drank more. His kids called, and he became mushy and sentimental, telling them how wonderful they were, but when they invited him to come for a visit he always said no. Griff drank more, yes, but mostly he sat around home all winter licking his wounds, feeling sorry for himself.

All of the love Griff once devoted to Mavis and Trixie, he now gave to his herd. Cattle were his life. They were his bread and butter and they provided what little nurturing his soul wrenched from an uncaring world.

Now, what used to be a lively walk had become a shuffle. His feet shuffled along barely off the ground as he grudgingly forced himself to endure each day. Everything he did he did slowly and apparently without purpose. He was sloppy. He was sloppy when he cooked; the can from his dinner of pork and beans still sat on the counter. He was sloppy when he mucked out his barn. He dressed sloppily—the same green pants, green work shirt, dirty long underwear both winter and summer. And his forty-odd extra pounds hung sloppily from his six-foot-five-inch frame.

Living alone these last years, he'd had no one immediately at hand upon whom he could vent his enormous anger, so he argued with his neighbours. Jake and his sister Elsa and his mom and dad were newcomers. Griff Webster had never said so much as a "how do you do" to them, with the exception of Jake, who was the spitting image of his own grandson, yet he had already made up his mind that he did not care for them. They were city folk, first off, living on a ranch. Not much of a ranch, mind you, but a hundred and sixty acres of pasture and hay fields and a barn and some other odd outbuildings and an old wooden clapboard house that was little better than a tent come winter. That was the first reason he disliked them, city folk imitating ranchers. Phonies.

The second reason was he'd never liked the last guy that lived there. The third and most important reason was he'd heard they were nursing a hurt coyote, that she had given birth to ten pups and that the Grant family was setting about the raising of those pups and letting them run free here, there and everywhere. Dumber city-type thinking Griff had never come across. It was, no two ways about it, insane. As he nursed yet another beer, Griff set about figuring out the best way to inform his new neighbours from the city of the true nature of the coyote and the sheer ridiculousness of what they were doing once and for all.

Chapter 8
Griff Webster Stops By

It had become habit for Jake to lie with his head at the end of his bed and look out the window before falling asleep. It was one of his favourite times, just looking into the darkness and listening to the quiet. This night the pole light was on in the yard. Jake looked at everything he could see in its circle of light—the shed, the chicken coop, the fence to the sheep pasture, the old out-house and toolshed. The first time he had done this was the night they arrived from the city, and then it scared him. There was no traffic noise, no activity, no neighbours. Everything he was used to was gone. He made a fruitless search that first night for something, anything, that was familiar. But there had just been this frightful darkness and this huge silence, both, it seemed, poised to devour him. Now, almost a year since they had moved in, things were better. Both the silence and the darkness were his friends now, and he was proud of this, proud that he no longer felt scared.

But tonight something wasn't right. He could feel it, and shortly he understood why. A pair of headlights crept into the yard below Jake's window and there appeared a black pickup. Jake recognized it immediately; it was the same pickup that Griff Webster had driven that day he and Willy were racing. There was a gun rack across the top of the seat with a rifle slung there, and their ornery neighbour was driving. From what he had heard of Griff Webster and considering the lateness of the hour, this could only be trouble.

As Jake watched the black pickup come to a stop in the yard, he felt uneasy. Perhaps this was because he knew what a loud, rough and complaining man Griff was. Perhaps it was the presence of the rifle. Jake wasn't sure, but whatever it was didn't matter, for now the man known to be miserable in all of his dealings with neighbours was in their yard. He had turned the lights off, and was just sitting there in his truck, staring at the house. He did not see Jake, barely twenty metres away, as he downed the last of a beer,

scrunched the can in his big fist and tossed it out the open window of the pickup onto the ground.

Griff Webster leaned out of his window, his chin resting on folded arms, and just stared. Jake went downstairs where his parents were watching television. He didn't want to tell his dad what was happening, but there was no choice. Jake had one of his uneasy feelings, a "bad hunch," he called it. He knew that his dad would be unhappy to be visited by their strange neighbour so late at night.

"Dad?" Jake said.

"What are you doing up, Son?"

"It's that neighbour, the one with the black truck. He's in the yard just sitting there."

Mr. G. jumped up as though he expected something terrible to happen. He hurried to the back door. When he stepped outside and walked toward the truck, he was wearing a dressing gown. Griff spoke first.

"Neighbour to the west." He did not offer his hand.

"Mr. Webster," Mr. G. said. "How are you?" Jake stood listening, just inside the door. The feeling was bigger now.

"Good. Real good."

"Good then."

"Good then. Never met you before, but I did

meet that fine boy of yours."

"Yes," Mr. G. replied cautiously, "he mentioned that."

"Yeah, well, this ain't a social call. I stopped by to tell you about my concern."

"Your concern?"

"That's right. Calving time. When calves get born. Springtime."

"I do know about that. We've got a few cows ourselves. Going to calve any day now."

"Well, maybe then you'll understand my problem."

"Just what is your problem, Mr. Webster?"

"My problem, see, is this here … you got your wild dogs. You got your wolves. And you got your coyotes. That's my problem."

"I see. You're worried about your newborn calves being taken by—"

"That's right. That's right. That's right. Being taken by wild dogs, by wolves and by coyotes. You see?"

"I think so."

"Well, now, I wonder about that."

Jake was remembering something that had happened years ago. They'd been drinking in the kitchen, his dad and his writer friend, back in Vancouver. This friend was the only man Mrs. G. had ever met who terrified her. She was right: there had been a fight that night and Jake had seen it happen. Jake's dad had thrown the man out and told him to never come back. Jake had never seen him again and he understood why: he knew what a firecracker Mr. G. could be.

Griff Webster's way with neighbours was well known too. The neighbours on the other side, the McGilvrays, though they had lived several years there, were no friendlier with him than the Grants. But knowing him to be hard-nosed and unreasonable only increased Mr. G.'s annoyance. Griff had said the word "neighbour" as though there were something vile crawling around the inside of his mouth, and then he had spit on the ground at Jake's dad's feet.

Mr. G. stood silent, trying to control himself. "I said, I wonder about that," Griff said.

"I heard you."

After a tense silence Griff Webster went on, "I mean to say, neighbour, I wonder could a neighbour really understand if in point of fact it's true what I hear?"

Mr. G. held his breath. Then he forced himself to breathe deeply and said, "I guess that depends on what it is you hear, Griff."

"Glad you asked. I hear tell you and yours is

nursing a coyote bitch lost her mate. That true?"

"I don't know if she has lost her mate or not, but we're nursing a coyote bitch, yes."

"Straight answer to a straight question, I like that."

"But you don't like the fact that we're helping a coyote. Right?"

"That'd be it, all right. So where you hiding them?"

"Where am I hiding them? I'm not hiding them anywhere."

Jake tightened up still more. Barely breathing, he kept looking at that rifle on the rack behind Griff's head.

"Okay, so you're not hiding them. Where they at then?"

Mr. G. stood about two metres away from the truck. The smell of his neighbour's beer-drenched breath hung between them in the still night air. He couldn't believe what he was hearing from this belligerent man, and suddenly he felt vulnerable standing there in his housecoat while Griff was basically challenging him to—to what? Mr. G. wasn't sure. He made up his mind.

"They're here, a bitch and ten pups. Exactly where is none of your business."

"Oh-oh," Jake muttered to himself. His dad

was getting madder and madder. Griff Webster, as big and as mean as he was, better watch out.

"Okay, city fella, that's your attitude, I'll just take a little look-see." He opened the truck door, and just as his big leg began to swing out Mr. G. stepped forward and kicked the door closed. "This is my property. You do not have my permission to snoop around."

"Well, now, don't that take all. Mr. City has got some life in him. Gotta say I like that."

The beer breath, all of a sudden, filled Mr. G.'s senses. He was revolted by the smell. And then he noticed the scrunched-up empty can on the ground.

He bent down and picked it up. "This, I believe, belongs to you." He reached into the open window of the pickup and dropped the scrunched-up beer can onto Griff Webster's lap. There had been a sip of beer still in there, and it drained onto his pants and soaked through them, and through the long underwear too, and as soon as he felt the wet against his skin, Griff said, "Why, you son of a bitch." He started to open the door again, and again Mr. G. slammed it shut, this time with both hands. Then he kept his hands on the door and leaned into his neighbour's drink-slackened face. When Mr. G. spoke, the sound of his voice was a command to listen and listen carefully and don't get any part of it wrong.

"Get off my land."

Webster was suddenly sober. He was thinking hard, you could see this in his face, and while he thought he stared stupidly at the sudden and unexpected change in his neighbour from the city. Whatever he had wanted this late-night visit to become, this wasn't it. He started his truck, backed up throwing gravel, then peeled forward. Mr. G. had to jump aside to escape the flying stones.

Jake waited a few counts to let his dad cool down.

"Dad?" he finally said.

"I was hoping you didn't hear that." He was so angry he was shaking.

"Are you okay?"

"All I could think was this drunk jerk is going to find Shadow and the pups and then he's going to start shooting. I couldn't let him out of that truck. You stay inside, Son. He might be back."

"But Shadow might need me. I have to go check on her."

"Not half as much as your mother and I do. You stay inside."

Jake's parents hugged when his dad came back inside. Jake waited while things calmed down, and then he said, "Can I just go out now then? Just for a minute, please?"

"One minute. I'll wait right here."

He ran out to the shed. Shadow was awake, watching. All the pups were asleep except the littlest one, Number Ten. Jake thought Shadow looked worried. He petted her. Concerned, maybe. He wondered if she really could understand what had just happened. His mom said Shadow understood everything. Everything that was said, everything that happened. "Maybe," he said to himself.

Jake's mom and dad sat at the kitchen table, a bottle of red wine in front of them and two glasses. Mr. G.'s dressing gown had fallen open, showing the heavy black hair on his chest.

"Night, Dad."

"Night, Son." He squeezed extra hard when he hugged his son goodnight.

Jake hurried upstairs and curled up on the end of his bed. He covered himself with the sleeping bag he had used when he slept with Shadow in the shed, and peered out the window. The pole light was still on — the entire yard was lit up, the shed where Shadow and her pups lay behind the stack of wood, his bike leaning against the granary, and the tire tracks where Griff Webster had peeled away.

Jake liked it best when things settled down, when everything was okay in the end. But, as he stared beyond the circle of light and into the darkness, he had the strong sense that this Griff Webster situation was far from over.

Chapter 9
Shadow Moves Out

Next morning, Saturday, Jake slept in. When he awoke and saw that it was nine o'clock, he dressed quickly and ran outside. As he crossed the yard to the shed, he pulled on his dad's parka. Mrs. G. was asleep on the cot and Shadow and all the puppies were asleep too. Shadow woke up and weakly wagged her tail, then seemed to fall into a trance, her eyes staring into nowhere. Jake tipped the baby bottle into Shadow's mouth and squeezed. Just then his mom woke up.

"Go back to sleep," Jake said. "I can do it."

"How long have you been here?"

"I just got here."

"Were they asleep?"

"Everybody was asleep. Shadow woke up

when I came."

"Oh, good. I woke up about seven feeling terrified that Shadow was dead. I could barely get a reaction out of her. So I heated some milk and tilted back her head and stuck the bottle as far into her mouth as I could and squirted."

"Wow! I was so tired I just couldn't wake up."

"Don't you go feeling bad. If it wasn't for you, none of these guys would be alive right now."

"You think?"

"Your father and I are very proud of you."

Jake glowed inside. He squeezed a bit harder on the bottle, emptying it into Shadow's mouth.

"Now you go in and put shoes and socks on. And make me a cup of tea, please, and heat up some more milk for Shadow. I'm going to try to get Number Ten to feed from his mother."

Jake came back wearing rubber boots and carrying a steaming cup of tea in one hand and a plate of cinnamon toast in the other.

"Will he do it?"

"Not a chance. He's not the least bit interested."

Jake handed her the tea and toast.

"This is great," she said. "Have you got socks on in those boots?"

How did she know?

"I have to get my hot chocolate anyway," he mumbled. Then he brought the baby bottle from the pocket of his dad's parka. "Here," and he ran back inside.

When Jake came back with a cup of hot chocolate and wearing socks in his rubber boots, the vet was there. He stood about three metres from Mrs. G.'s cot.

"It's okay. I'm not coming any closer."

When he took a step toward her, Shadow stood up and snarled at him. Mrs. G. tried calming Shadow down, but she would have none of it. That man was not getting near her and he was not getting near her puppies.

"Alright, alright, I came to look at pigs anyway." And he hurried off toward the barn.

"Wow. Shadow stood up!"

"Did she ever!"

"Let's try this," Jake said. Shadow was lying back down, exhausted from defending herself and her family from the vet. She was panting, but Jake thought she looked pleased with herself. He held a single round of dried dog food up to her nose. Shadow sniffed it and then her tongue shot out and it was gone. Jake held up another one. Same thing. Then he held the bowl up and Shadow pushed it down with her nose, so he set it on the ground. Immediately she sat up and ate.

Jake and his mom watched. She was going to make it after all. Jake wanted to shout for joy. He felt that Shadow was a hero giving birth to ten pups, and that he himself had played a small part in her heroism. He wanted to yell as loud as he could. He didn't yell, though. He thought he might yell some other time when he was alone.

In a few more days the puppies were moving around, and at about ten days their eyes opened and they could see the world for the first time. At least, they could see the woodshed, anyway. Shadow was so proud. And she got prouder and prouder as she got stronger. As she became more independent, she was grumpy with everyone except Jake and his mom. If Elsa or Mr. G. came by, Shadow would hurry to her feet and stand between them and the pups. She didn't say "Stop," of course, but it was easy to tell what she wanted. Shadow had a way of putting "No" on her face that was like seeing what she was thinking.

The only problem was Number Ten. Mrs. G. and Jake tried everything they could think of to get him to feed from a teat, but he just plain refused. "Most stubborn animal I have ever met,"

Mrs. G. said. But hold a bottle up to him and Ten would feed constantly. Soon he was the littlest and the fattest of them all. It was more work keeping Number Ten alive than Shadow and all of the other pups combined.

Shadow was soon strong enough to go out each night to hunt. She would come back and regurgitate a rabbit onto the ground in the shed. She had to carry it somehow, so she carried it in her stomach. The pups knew what to do. All Shadow did was nudge here and there to make sure everybody got some. That was all there was to it. Except, of course, for Number Ten, who sniffed the rabbit and touched it with her tongue, but refused to eat.

When Shadow couldn't bring enough home to feed all her pups, she allowed them to eat dry dog food. But she didn't like this. She always watched and when she thought they had had enough, she made them stop. And the only people who could fill the food bowls or the milk bowls were Jake or his mom. Shadow kept everybody else away.

Jake knew she wasn't tame like a dog. Shadow was a wild coyote. And although he knew this, it was hard to accept that she would someday take all her pups back to the bush and he would be left with just listening for her howls.

Mr. G. tried to straighten him out on that. "You did a wonderful thing, you and your mother. I have no doubt you saved Shadow's life. She could never have cared for those ten pups if she still had that collar on. Assuming she survived the birthing, which is doubtful. But you have to accept that she's wild. She came from the wild, and she'll go back there. You'll have a friend out there in the bush. Think of it that way."

When Jake thought it through, that was enough. He and Shadow would be friends, wherever she was.

Soon Shadow wouldn't let anyone feed her pups. And not even Jake could pick a puppy up anymore. Shadow was taking control.

And she was staying away all night. When she was gone, the pups stayed inside the shed. Not even Mikey took off on his own. When she came back in the morning, she regurgitated food onto the ground. They loved this. Number Ten, of course, would still have nothing to do with it. While his brothers and sisters ate the regurgitated meat, Ten sat back and watched. Shadow wouldn't let either Jake or his mom near Ten, so they had to feed him at night when Shadow was away. Sometimes if Ten was hungry enough he would drink milk from a bowl, though. Then, when Shadow came back from hunting, she sniffed around the entrance to the shed and around the bowl itself, and she didn't look very happy about it.

The pups grew quickly and moved around and got into things on their own. It was okay to play fight and chase each other, but if one of them got too far from the shed, Shadow appeared out of nowhere, picked the puppy up by the scruff of his neck and took him back with the others. Shadow would stay around for a while, nudging puppies and sniffing them to see if anything had happened that she didn't already know about.

Then one day Jake came home from school and Shadow and all ten pups were gone. He looked everywhere he could think of — behind the barn, behind the shed. He walked back to the bush and called and called. No Shadow. No pups. He wondered how Shadow could possibly feed and protect ten puppies, and he wondered if she would come back if she ever needed his help. Then he remembered how Shadow came to him the first time. "Maybe I should try it again," he said to himself.

Jake went inside and poured a big glass of milk. He made a sack with the belly of his shirt and filled it with his favourite cookie, homemade peanut butter. Then he went out and sat in that same spot facing the sheep pasture. He took a big drink of milk and bit into his first cookie.

It was a beautiful day. The aspen along the laneway had fully greened up. The leaves were twisting upside down and then back again like they do, alternately glistening with sunlight and then almost disappearing into the intensity of the light in the sky.

He could smell the heat, smell the dust from the road, and he smelled the grass beneath him. There were so many things to smell, he wondered how Shadow did it, having such a sensitive nose.

Then, as though thinking of her brought her to him, Shadow appeared behind him. Jake knew she was there. Without bothering to look and make sure, he held a cookie out to the side.

"Here," he said.

Shadow knew what it was and didn't hesitate. She stepped forward and gently took the cookie in her mouth. Jake felt her cold wet nose against his hand. Then Shadow moved in front of him and sat down. She was staring at him, and she wasn't eating the cookie, but holding it lightly in her mouth.

Something passed between them, from

Shadow to Jake, and from Jake to Shadow. He knew that his father was right.

Shadow turned and trotted off like coyotes do, but she didn't go back to the bush like Jake thought she would. She went straight to the tall grass by the old tractor. "Dummy," he said to himself. He hadn't thought to look there.

When Jake got there, Shadow still had the cookie in her mouth. The pups were jumping at her, all trying to be where they thought she would drop it. The problem Shadow was having was dividing one peanut butter cookie into ten pieces. Jake still had several left. He held them for Shadow to see. She looked, then let hers fall to the ground. He did the same with his, and there was a scramble of pups until the tiniest morsel was licked up.

There was one pup who wasn't scrambling, though, and that was Number Ten. He sat back from the jumble of puppies and watched. Jake wasn't sure, but he thought that maybe Ten had lost a bit of weight. He bent down to pick Ten up, and Shadow stepped between them. Jake stood back. He looked at Shadow, who dipped her head and looked away. Jake understood. Shadow didn't feel good about challenging him, but she was determined.

"It's okay, girl," he said.

Then he turned and walked back to that same spot facing the sheep pasture. He had given the pups all his cookies, but wanted to finish the milk. He raised the glass to his mouth, and just as he was drinking he noticed the bug. Not fast enough, though. Jake spit it out and felt around inside his mouth with his tongue. When he was sure the bug wasn't in there, he emptied the glass into his mouth, hesitated and then swallowed it down.

Chapter 10
Ten-Eighty

The next day Jake felt lost. He wandered about the ranch, getting back in touch with the animals he had been ignoring since Shadow's arrival. The pigs were finally getting around to eating the thistles in their outside pen. Thistles were the only vegetation remaining. They must not like them, but if that was all there was, then eventually they would dig away at them and eat the roots. In his brief time living on a ranch, he had come to the conclusion that pigs would eat just about anything. He remembered Elsa's pie, though. It was her first try at lemon meringue. It tasted odd, so they threw it into the pigpen. The pigs wouldn't touch it. Then there was the dead chicken. He and his dad had come out to do the chores and there was a dead chicken in the feeder. Mr. G. tossed the carcass into the pigpen. It was gone in seconds. "So there it is. Even a dead chicken tastes better than Elsa's pie."

Jake was beginning to think like a rancher. He didn't just see grass. He noticed which growth sheep ate and which they left behind, and the same for cattle. Summer was coming on and there was a feeling of easy living about the ranch. The only feed the sheep and the cows would need for the next few months was growing in the fields. All he and his dad had to do was move the herds from pasture to pasture to make sure there was no over-grazing. The rest of the work at that relaxed time of year involved repairs to machinery and build-ings, work without pressure.

Jake sat down by the empty glass that he had left there the day before. There were several bugs in it now. He watched them, then spit into the glass and spit again, then poured it all onto the ground.

Jake wanted Shadow to come to him. He saw her in his mind with that calm but curious look on her face. He saw her holding a cookie in her mouth. But the real Shadow didn't come. He called, "Shadow, here Shadow," thinking that she might be lying down in the tall grass around the old tractor. Nothing. Then he reminded himself of what his dad had said. No matter what, he and Shadow were friends. This would have to do for now.

It was Saturday night, and Willy slept over. The foamy Jake had slept on in the woodshed was on the floor in his bedroom. Willy was asleep there. Sound asleep. Snoring. Until he met Willy, Jake didn't think kids snored, but Will was a real honker.

Lying at the foot of his bed, Jake watched his dad come into the house from the barn. The pole light stayed on. After Griff's visit, Mr. G. wasn't taking any chances. Even though Shadow and the pups were gone, he felt sure that they were still close by.

Then he saw her. Jake hurried downstairs, pulled his dad's parka around him and stepped quietly outside.

"Hi, Shadow."

She was sitting just on the edge of the circle of light thrown by the pole lamp. Her bushy tail wagged once.

Jake was about to speak again, but something made him hold back. Then it came to him in a flash why Shadow was there. He sat down on the ground about three metres from her. Shadow came smartly to him, sat down and leaned into

Jake's chest. His arms encircled her. They hugged for several seconds. Then Jake's arms fell to his sides. Shadow looked directly into his eyes, then bounded off, over the fence and out of sight.

She'd come back to say good-bye. Jake felt sad, but good. He went back to his room, stepped over Willy and into bed and fell immediately into a deep sleep.

A few hours later he wakened with a start. Something wasn't right. Jake moved to the window at the foot of his bed and looked outside. The pole light was still on, but something moved on the edge of the darkness. Jake could barely make out the figure of a man.

"Hey, Will, wake up." Jake had to shake her, she was so hard to break out of sleep. "Wake up. There's somebody outside." Willy shook herself awake, then they both peered out the window.

"Son of a gun."

The figure briefly came into the light, just long enough to duck into the woodshed and out again.

"That's Griff. I'll bet you anything." She moved toward the door.

"Where you going?" Jake said.

"Let's go find out what he's up to."

Willy was so awake all of a sudden, and so keen to get right into whatever it was that was going on, Jake could only follow along. If his dad knew Griff Webster had come into his yard again, there would be trouble—big trouble. But he couldn't think about that just now. He and Willy stole silently downstairs, through the darkened house to the mud room. Jake slipped his bare feet into rubber boots and shrugged his dad's parka on over his peejays. Willy pulled on her runners. She had peejays on, too.

"Better put this on," Jake whispered. He handed her a lumberjack shirt of his dad's. Then they crouched beneath the window and watched.

"What do you think?"

"We can't go out here," Willy replied. "He'll see us for sure. Let's go out the other way."

They moved silently through the house and out the front door. They kept to the dark and stayed low, circling around the back of the shed. Willy peered around the corner of the woodshed, then immediately pulled back.

"Holy cripes! He's right there," she whispered.

They both looked. Griff Webster was standing at the fence, looking into the field. He was carrying a sack. He leaned over the fence and set the sack down on the other side. Then he crossed the fence himself, stepping onto the bottom rail and swinging his big leg over. He moved gracefully for a man of his size. Now he picked up the sack and started across the field toward the old tractor.

Jake and Willy went down on hands and knees and crept to the fence. When Griff tossed the sack into the field and crossed over, he was less than six metres from where they crouched.

Griff walked about ten steps into the field and then dumped the contents of the sack onto the ground and tossed the sack aside. Then he walked along the fence, staying well clear of the lighted yard. Jake and Willy were quickly over the fence and following behind him. When Griff Webster turned onto the laneway and walked along it to the road, Willy said, "He's got his truck up at the road. There's no sense in following."

"What's he up to, do you think?" Jake asked.

Willy turned and, walking normally now, headed back to that sack. "I'll tell you in a sec," she said.

She bent over, looked carefully at it and, even though it was dark, it was easy to see what it was. Guts. Animal guts, probably cow. Jake looked, too.

"Holy smokes," he said. "Offal." It was a new

word he'd come across in the coyote book he'd got from the library.

"Yeah, but there's something wrong." Willy peered closely at the gut pile, her eyes about twenty centimetres from the rotting flesh.

"Why, that dirty s.o.b.," she said.

"What?"

"Ten-Eighty. This thing is poison." She dug a capsule out of the flesh and held it up for Jake to see.

Ten-Eighty was a compound poison in capsule form. It was said that Ten-Eighty worked only on canines. It would kill a dog, a wolf or a coyote, but wouldn't harm a crow, and wouldn't harm any animal that fed on the carcass of the canine originally killed by it.

Jake ran to the fence, jumped it and ran to the house. He disappeared inside and within seconds reappeared with a flashlight. He had to hurry in case the pups got to the gut pile and Willy couldn't hold them all off. He didn't even know for sure if Shadow or the pups knew the gut pile was there, but he wasn't taking any chances. He ran to the barn for a shovel, then climbed back over the fence. No coyotes. Good.

"We have to burn it," Willy said. "There might be more."

The pups would have no chance. Jake and Willy shovelled the guts back into the sack, cleaned the ground carefully, then carried the sack to the yard where there was a burn barrel, a forty-five-gallon drum with the top cut off and holes drilled into the sides. They dropped the sack into the barrel and then got small pieces of wood from the shed, and some gasoline. They lay the wood on top of the gut bag and along the sides, then sprinkled it all with gas. While the gas soaked in, Jake went into the house for matches.

He came back out with the matches and two oranges, one of which he gave to Willy. He paused, feeling for wind. There was none that he could detect. He struck a match and tossed it into the barrel. Before the match hit the gasoline-soaked kindling, Jake and Willy made a fast withdrawal. When the gas exploded into flame, they were far enough back that all they felt was the heat on their skin. The fire burned furiously, then settled down, and soon they could smell burning flesh, a sickening smell that made Jake's heart sink. Jake thought they should maybe go to bed, afraid he might wake up one of his parents, but he knew he wouldn't settle. Willy, though, was ready to go back to dreamland.

"I'm hitting the hay." Then, after a few steps,

she turned back and said, "Somebody has to do something about him."

"Yeah," Jake agreed. "I know." Then he hurried to add, "Will?"

"Yeah?"

"Let's keep quiet about this. If Dad finds out, things could get real ugly."

"Okay. I hope you know what you're doing." Willy went inside.

Jake sat down far enough away that he couldn't smell the burnt flesh. There was barely any smoke at all, and the only firelight he could see was through the air holes that had been drilled in the barrel sides. He snugged the big coat close around himself. He broke the orange into sections, the way he always did, and popped the first one into his mouth. He was sure he could solve this problem. He just wasn't sure how.

Chapter 11
Number Ten

The night Jake and Willy burned Griff Webster's gut pile, Shadow and all the pups left the tall grass around the old tractor for good. Where they went Jake didn't know. Whether or not they were okay he didn't know. He filled the enormous gap left in his life by reading everything he could find about coyotes. He knew more than anybody else around about them, more than his dad, more than Willy, yet this knowing didn't bring Shadow or any of the puppies back. They were gone. Probably forever. He might never see any of them again. But there remained this one connection, the eerie, majestic howling that serenaded anyone in the Cariboo who bothered to listen. Although you might hear a coyote howl anytime,

99

day or night, at the Grant ranch the serenading seemed to intensify just after dark.

It became Jake's habit after Shadow left to sit atop the fence between their yard and the first field and listen. The howling fascinated him. There were so many coyote howls and they seemed so close. But mostly he was fascinated because he felt that he understood what some of those howls were saying. Coyotes howl, yes, virtually all of them, but nobody has been able to figure out what, if anything, is being said when a coyote howls.

Most of the howls that Jake heard he didn't understand either. They were beautiful and sometimes spooky, but the howling didn't mean anything to him. Except when it came from Shadow. When Shadow howled, Jake knew instantly that it was her. The howling might sound exactly the same as the last one, but he knew who it was because every time Shadow howled Jake felt a vibration in the centre of his chest. He felt her presence in such a strong and clear way that he would peer into the darkness expecting her to be there.

He could never tell which direction the howling came from, though. It was like trying to pinpoint the source of a sound heard across water. But he always knew what she was saying. After taking her pups back into the bush, Shadow was telling the world how difficult life was feeding all her pups without a mate. Perhaps there was a male coyote whose mate had been lost just as hers had been. As Jake listened to the howls that came after Shadow's, he felt certain that one of them was offering himself to her, but he couldn't tell for sure. He did sense a relaxation in Shadow, though, a new certainty, and this made him feel good, too.

Understanding Shadow's howling was something Jake didn't speak about to anyone else, not even Willy. And even though he knew that no one else could interpret coyote howling, he was sure of his understanding, like his mind and Shadow's mind were linked together. Like whenever Shadow thought something, Jake knew what it was. It was almost as though his mind and hers operated within each other. Could this be or was he just crazy? And if he was crazy, then why could he understand with so much sureness, and why were those particular howls vibrating inside his chest like they did?

No matter, he decided, there was something more important happening. Shadow had a problem, but he couldn't figure out what it was. He was upset with himself for not getting it, until he realized that Shadow herself was confused. It made sense then that he wouldn't understand either. Shadow was having a problem with one of her pups, and she didn't know how to solve it.

"Jake," his mom called. "It's past bedtime."

"I know."

"Aren't you coming in?"

"In a minute."

About five minutes later his mom brought him a glass of milk and a piece of carrot cake. "I thought you might like to have your snack out here."

"Thanks."

Ever since the birthing, his parents were giving him more room. Jake noticed right away and he liked it a lot. Before Shadow and the pups came along, he wouldn't have been allowed to sit outside so long after bedtime. But he felt this new respect coming from his mom and dad.

He drank half the milk and ate all the carrot cake except a single bite. Then he finished the milk and dropped the empty glass onto the ground on the yard side of the fence. The last bite of cake he set on the rail beside him.

Jake was thinking about how his mom hadn't bugged him about bedtime. She had always bugged him about bedtime before. And tonight she even brought his snack outside. Nice. And then he saw her, sitting about three metres in front of him.

"Hey, Shadow!" Jake said aloud.

As soon as he said her name, Shadow moved farther into the field. Then she turned and looked back at Jake. She wanted him to follow. He dropped off the fence and went after her. She led him to the tall grass surrounding the old tractor. Shadow stepped into the grass and sat down. She looked at the ground in front of her, then she looked at Jake, back and forth like this a couple of times. Jake was confused. In the darkness, even Shadow herself was just a bare outline. Then he heard a whimper. He separated the grass in front of Shadow and there lay Number Ten.

Shadow and Jake stared at each other. Jake sensed that she wanted him to take Number Ten away with him. He bent down to pick Ten up, pausing to see if Shadow objected. When she didn't, Jake picked Number Ten up and held him against his chest. Ten didn't seem to recognize him. His eyes were closed. Jake could feel his ribs. No more did Number Ten have a fat belly and a tail that always wagged. As Jake petted Ten and tried to get him to open his eyes, Shadow ran off.

When Jake came into the kitchen cradling

Number Ten in his arms, Mr. and Mrs. G. were sitting at the table drinking a glass of wine. As soon as she saw Ten, Jake's mom gasped, "Oh, my God." She took him into her arms and held him close against her chest as she put milk on the stove to heat.

Jake sat at the table and watched.

"Where did you get him?" his dad asked.

"Shadow brought him to me when I was on the fence."

"Amazing," Mr. G. said.

"Oh, my God," Mrs. G. kept saying. She put water on to sterilize a baby bottle.

Jake looked at the kitchen clock. It was almost an hour past his usual bedtime. Although no one had really said so, it seemed that bedtime wasn't bedtime anymore. Even though school was almost out, and he was writing exams all this week, bedtime seemed to be whenever he thought best. Sitting at the table watching his mom prepare the bottle, he felt strangely peaceful. As sick as Ten was, Jake knew he would be okay. This knowing wasn't words in his head, but was a sureness, a certainty that flowed through his body. And this was connected somehow to his no longer having a set bedtime. He felt great.

His mom filled the sterilized bottle with warm

milk and then dabbed some onto her finger. She held the finger up to Ten's nose. At first there was no reaction, but then Ten came alive, as though suddenly remembering how to do it. His eyes opened and his tongue shot out. He licked the milk from her finger and continued licking after the milk was gone. She quickly slipped the nipple into his mouth. Jake could see Ten's throat get tighter and then relax and then tighten again as he sucked at the bottle.

"Can I?"

Mrs. G. passed Ten and the fast-emptying bottle to him. The pup kept drinking hard, while Jake's mom went into the back kitchen for the canvas bag she carried him in when he was first born.

"It won't be long," she said. "Better put him in this."

"Could I put him in a box in my room with some newspapers in it?"

"I guess you think he's going to be okay?"

"Ten'll be fine. He just misses us."

Exams started the day after Number Ten came home. Jake had been worried about them, but he was actually better prepared than he'd realized. He had wanted to do well so that he could forget about school for the whole summer, and that was exactly what happened.

Over that same period Ten ate almost all the time, just like he used to. After a few days of the bottle, he eagerly devoured dried dog food. Mrs. G. thought he might like raw meat, so she tried to give him some, but Ten would have none of it.

"He's different," she said. "Most peaceful animal I've ever seen."

Ten had three loves, Mrs. G., Jake and food. By the end of two weeks he was thirty centimetres tall and fat and happy.

Then one night Jake woke up suddenly. He thought at first something was wrong. He checked Ten, fast asleep in his box beside the bed. Then he moved to the foot of his bed and looked outside.

The yard light was on. Jake wasn't surprised to see Shadow sitting on her haunches, looking intently up at his window. He wondered what it was she wanted, and shortly after wondering this he knew. Number Ten. Shadow wanted him back.

Jake tried sending her "No" thoughts, just as he knew she sent hers to him, but she refused to budge. In spite of Shadow's stubbornness, though, something told Jake everything would be okay.

He picked up the box with the sleeping Number Ten in it and carried it out to the yard.

Shadow hadn't moved. Jake set the box down between them. Ten was awake now, but still lying down. Jake backed away and watched.

Shadow sniffed Ten all over. Then she sniffed him all over again. Ten licked his mother's nose, but otherwise he just lay there. Finally Shadow moved away a few steps and then turned back toward Ten and said, "Come on!" Ten held fast. He watched Shadow. He wagged his tail a bit, and his ears drooped down, but otherwise he didn't move.

Shadow sat back down. Her eyes moved back and forth from Ten to Jake. Then finally she turned and bounded across the yard and was over the fence. Jake peered after her into the blackness. Then he picked up Number Ten's box and went back to his room.

Jake put the box in its place and climbed back into bed. He had a social studies exam next day. He asked himself two questions that he thought might be on the exam and immediately came up with the answers. Then he remembered that last bite of carrot cake. "Ah," he said to himself, "feed the bugs," and he immediately dropped off to sleep.

Chapter 12
A Dead Coyote

Ten was frisking here and there, trying to weasel food from anyone at the table. Jake was happy, and his happiness was catching, so the whole family felt good. He had told them about Shadow coming by and about Ten saying no. The possibility of Ten returning to the bush once he got better had been on everyone's mind, and now they all felt relieved. But Jake still kept quiet about the Ten-Eighty and the gut pile Griff Webster had dumped in the field. Burning garbage was one of Jake's chores. The next day he had gone through the house and barn and had filled the barrel and then set it alight. Neither his dad nor his mom was at all suspicious.

He had a few minutes before catching the bus

to school. He wanted to hurry through break-fast, then take Ten out for a walk before leaving. Elsa wanted to go also. Although Number Ten was more Jake's pet than anyone else's in the family, she spent as much time with him as she could. Mrs. G. was eager to have Ten all to herself. She knew that soon the kids would be gone and Mr. G. would be leaving to work outside.

Mr. G. stood to look out the window. Some-one was coming. As soon as he saw the black pickup, he knew who it was. He felt tense, re-membering his miserable neighbour's last visit. And he remembered also how close he had come then to losing his temper and saying or doing something he would one day regret. Jake looked too. When he saw who it was, he was afraid it might come out about the Ten-Eighty. Mr. G. hurried outside and was waiting when the truck stopped in the yard.

Griff Webster stepped out and, without speak-ing, hurried to the back of the truck. He dropped the tailgate, then pulled a dead animal onto the ground.

"Know what that is?" he spat.

"I do."

"Shot him this morning. Head shot. Too bad. He didn't suffer none."

"Good."

"Figured it might be yours. Knowin' your fondness for 'em."

Jake had slipped out of the kitchen and stood by the back door, his eyes fixed on the carcass. It was a coyote. He feared that it might be Shadow. But it was a male, and a large male, so neither was it one of the pups. But his relief was small. He felt that rock of fear start to harden in the pit of his stomach. Ten tried to push outside but Jake kept him in, hoping that he wouldn't make any noise. Jake stared hard. He didn't understand, and was trying desperately to do so. Words were being spoken, but they barely registered in his mind.

"Tell you what I seen yesterday. This same son of a bitch walkin' right in with my herd. I seen it with my own eyes. Movin' with 'em, sniffin' 'em out. Lookin' for the best one."

"Did he chase any of them?"

"He was sizin' 'em up."

"He didn't pay any more attention to the calves than to the cows?"

"Fessin' the situation out, I tell you. Layin' down plans for once it got dark. Coyotes is too smart to hunt down a calf in broad daylight. It's always at night. Or early mornin' like this son of a bitch."

"I'm not so sure. I do know that a coyote will walk with a herd so when the cows scare up a mouse or a gopher he can chase it down. But there's a big difference between eating a gopher and eating a calf. A mighty big difference. Studies have been done that show the number-one food of coyotes is rabbits and the number-two food is carrion."

Griff Webster got suddenly angrier. "Okay, Mr. City Fella, I'll tell you right here and now. Coyotes, two, three, four of 'em, whatever, will stalk a herd. Stay with it for days sometimes, waitin' for a chance. That chance comes and two or three of 'em will get in close on one of the cows, like they're going to attack any minute. Cow gets all nervous and what happens, other coyote makes a quick dash into the herd, and quicker'n you can spit, he rips the arsehole out of one of the calves. Then they all take off. They take off, see, but they don't leave, they're hangin' around the edges of the herd, keeping an eye on that wounded calf.

"First few days the cows'll protect the calf, then they figure out the little fella's going to die anyway and they more or less abandon her. So they walk away from the poor sufferin' critter and who shows up? That's right, yer peace-lovin' coyotes.

That, city fella, is what your fancy-pants scientists call carrion."

"I've never heard that before."

"Well, you've heard it now. And there ain't a lot of meat on a calf. They'll all feed on her, but they'll be back at her in a day or two."

"Have you ever seen this?"

"Well, no, but I know a guy swears he has."

Jake ducked inside. "Mom, what's carrion?" She was watching and listening at the kitchen window.

"Carrion is dead animals."

"Do you think he's right?"

"I've always thought of carrion as something they just come across, not something that they kill."

Jake went back outside. Griff Webster was getting angrier still.

"Fact or no, you is carin' for a mess o' coyotes?"

"Not any more, but we did that, yes. At the moment we've got one pup left and it looks like he'll be staying with us."

"Alright then," he said in triumph. "Fact or no, coyotes stick where they was born, provided there's enough food for 'em?"

"Agreed."

"Fact or no, coyotes eat meat?"

"They do."

"Fact or no, coyotes have been known to kill deer?"

"Some, a few, yes, but not many, though, and not usually."

"Fact nonetheless. Okay now, fact or no, coyotes have been known to kill calves?"

"Maybe. Nobody seems to have sure proof. Could be wolves. Could be wild dogs."

"Dammit, man, I just finished tellin' ya. What kind of proof you need?"

"Yes, but you also said you've never seen it yourself."

"The fella tol' me that is honest as the day is long."

"Well," Jake's dad said, "if what you say is true, then I don't see why I haven't read something about it. I've read a fair bit about coyotes."

"Read, my ass. You and your damn books." He got back into the truck.

Mr. G. indicated the carcass. "You're not leaving that there, are you?"

"I am." And with that he peeled out the lane.

Jake went to his dad and his dad put his arm around him. He thought again that maybe he should tell him about the Ten-Eighty, but decided against it.

"That son of a bitch," his dad said.

Jake stared at the carcass. It was fascinating in a weird kind of way. There was a bullet hole in the head, but hardly any blood.

Mr. G. got the Massey-Ferguson, their tractor with the front-end loader on it, and scooped the carcass into the bucket. He got a shovel from the shed, put it into the bucket also, then headed the old red tractor toward the bush.

Jake stood watching. He couldn't get the image of that dead coyote from his mind. Then his mom said, "Jake, you'd better hurry or you'll miss the bus."

Elsa came out the door carrying her lunch and books and his also. He brushed passed her to go in and say good-bye to Ten. He explained to him that he would be back at three-thirty and he reminded his mom to not let Ten out of her sight. Then he went back outside and picked up the books and lunch that Elsa had set down. He walked wide around where the dead coyote had lain, then ran out the lane to catch up with his sister.

Chapter 13
Coyote Summer

The aspen along the Grants' laneway had fully leafed up, and the springtime green of the hay fields and pastures was slowly giving way to a summer tan. By the end of June it had stopped raining, and probably wouldn't rain again all summer.

School was out at last. Jake passed easily into grade seven and was enjoying his first full summer on the ranch. For the first month he went one evening a week to his bike-repair course in town. He helped his dad with the chores every day, and there was other work, too, real work, like helping Mr. G. build a workshop, and feeding animals, and mucking out the barn, and, of course, the haying.

And Jake was enjoying his parents' new way of letting him make his own decisions. He loved having no set bedtime, and he loved doing work around the ranch. After all, Willy had been feeding the animals and mucking out the barn for years. Jake and Willy rode into town, eleven kilometres each way, as often as they wanted, and Jake joined the Four-H cattle club. At first, when he realized he could do what he wanted, he rode to town every day for five days in a row. But this became boring. The town kids that he saw were just hanging out and talking big, that's all.

Whenever Jake went to town, Number Ten always scooted along beside his bike until Jake got to the end of their lane, and there he would lie down and wait for his master to come back. After an hour or so Ten would trot down to the house for a drink and, if he was lucky, dog biscuits. He loved milk bones. Usually he was lucky, meaning Mrs. G. was around the kitchen. Once refreshed and satisfied, he would go back to the end of the lane, lie down in the tall grass and wait for Jake to come home.

Waiting was always interesting. First and before anything else he smelled things on the air. If a breeze was blowing then so much the better, for then he would smell things from far away, who knows how far, and these were always exciting smells to come by. The smells were overwhelming at times. Ten would have to toss his head through the air to clear his nostrils, or just close his mind to the many smells that meant nothing to him. He was waiting, of course, to smell or to hear or to see Jake. This is what he wanted. Waiting was a pleasure to Ten, for at the end of the waiting he always got the best reward possible: Jake would be home.

Jake loved to turn into their lane off the road to town and see Ten leap up from the tall grass and jump up and down and all around and generally take a fit he was so happy. Jake would get off his bike and play, tossing Ten away, and Ten would come back for more. Jake loved petting him and talking to him while Ten sniffed Jake all over to find out what he had been up to. Then he coasted the rest of the way to the house with Ten close beside him, happy and full of mischief. When they got to the house, it was snack time. Milk always, and cookies usually, but sometimes cake or a sandwich. Jake's mom had told him so often not to feed Ten too much people food, but he always gave him a couple of bites of whatever he was having.

One day, after splitting kindling for their fireplace, Jake, with Ten trotting along beside him, went looking for Mr. G. where he was bailing hay. The night before, Jake's dad had said how proud he was about the way his son was changing since the move. He said he would let Jake decide how to spend his time that first summer. Had he been raised on a ranch like his friend Willy, he would long ago have taken his place in the work to be done. But Jake was raised in the city and, although he had chores, there was an end to housework, while ranch work went on forever. Mr. G. had told Jake he could have until the end of his first full summer to pitch in on his own, then he said he would be laying the work on him a bit more heavily.

Jake thought about this a lot. In the city, he'd just wanted to play sports and go exploring. But ranch life was different. Willy worked practically all the time, and she seemed so much more capable than Jake was. After taking some time to think things over, he decided that he would work too, that he would take his place in the day-to-day running of the ranch, no less important than anyone else in the family.

Jake's dad was driving the tractor with the bailer on behind, eating up the neat rows of raked hay and spitting out the small, sixty-pound bales which now dotted the field. On the edge of the field was the stooker. His mom rode this when she had time, but she was busy with the first batch of jam of the season. The stooker sat idle. Jake knew how it worked. It was attached behind the bailer and someone stood on it. As the bales came out of the bailer, he stacked them up till there were five in a stook, then he pulled a lever and the platform dropped down and there the stook sat in the field. It was easier to come along with a wagon and pick up a stook than to have to stop at each bale. Jake knew his dad would be working long after dark to get the hay in, in case it rained. He looked up at the sky and thought it looked iffy. Maybe it would rain, maybe not. Jake wondered what his dad had meant when he said he could use some help. He went over to a bale and lifted. Heavy, too heavy. He thought a bit, then he and Ten ran after the tractor. His dad saw them coming and stopped.

Jake was quiet as he spoke. His dad couldn't hear over the engine noise so had to ask him to speak up.

"I said, why don't I drive the tractor and you can ride the stooker?" Then he added, "I can't lift the bales very well."

"Young man, that's the best idea I've heard all day."

It was a John Deere tractor, green, several years old and it had a canopy to keep off the worst of the sun. Jake had never driven one before. He climbed up into the driver's seat and his dad gave him his one and only lesson.

"Two ranges," he said, "high and low. Four forward gears in each range, one reverse. Low range is for bull work, like plowing, pulling stumps maybe. High range is for lighter work. This is pretty light so we use high range, second gear. Depends on the tractor, of course, and how bumpy the field is. Now the tractor is stopped, so the gearbox is in neutral. Always put it in neutral when you stop. You can leave it in whatever range you're in, though. Now this back here is the power take-off. It turns the bailer itself. You hear me holler, what you do is shove in the clutch and at the same time shut down the power take-off. It's off now, so why don't you start her up."

Jake levered the PTO into action, then off again.

"Good boy.

"Now the clutch. Put it in, this is the clutch, this is the brake. Put the clutch in, choose your gear, then ease the clutch out. Easy, easy. Try it first without being in gear."

Jake eased out the clutch.

"That's it," his dad said. "Smooth, smooth. Now at a certain point you're going to start to move. What a lot of people do when that happens is slow or speed up their release. Don't. Smooth and easy. It's important because you can jerk the load off, or worse still, me." He laughed, then stepped back.

Jake chose first gear, high range, then eased out the clutch and everything started to move, and then he finished with the clutch, smooth and easy. Ten yipped. His dad smiled. "You're a natural. Just remember I'm standing back here, and the reason I'm safe is because you're driving safely and you're paying attention. Let's give her a go."

Jake stopped and put the tractor in neutral while his dad got on behind him. Then he put it in second and eased out the clutch just like his dad said and drove back to the stooking platform. He got as close to it as he could without having to use reverse, then got off and helped his dad slide the stooker over, line it up, then drop the pin through the drawbar and the tongue of the stooker, attaching it behind the bailer. His dad stood on the platform and Jake headed them to where he had left off that row of raked hay.

Spread through everything he did was the wonderful smell of fresh cut hay. Better after it had lain in the field drying. Best with the raking, probably. It made him feel like he was living on top of the world, that smell. Like what he was doing was the one right thing for him to be doing at that time and place. He loved it.

That was the first of many hours Jake would spend that summer on the tractor. Willy came and helped out. Willy, of course, already knew how to drive. She drove for the first time when she was six. Jake truly was a natural. He was cautious and he didn't move until he had checked everything over. He was never in a hurry, and he never lost patience.

Ten loved tractor work, too. Especially haying, because whatever part of haying Jake was doing, mowing, raking, bailing, stooking or loading bales onto the wagon, mice were always stirred up and Ten loved to chase mice. He walked behind and when a mouse started scurrying he would run the mouse down and hold it with his front paw. The mouse would squirm and kick and squeak, and then Ten would let it go and chase it again. Sometimes he would take the squeaking mouse in his mouth and toss it into the air and watch it fall. With luck he could chase the same mouse for an hour. Often, though, the mouse got tired of running and just sat there quivering, and then Ten would be off to chase up another one.

There were also the daily chores. Jake fed the chickens and pigs every morning. Chickens were easy—pellets—while pigs would eat practically anything. Slop from the kitchen, feed from the co-op, and they grazed too. Cattle and sheep were mostly grazing in summer. He filled their water troughs, though, and made sure there was still something left of the salt block. He looked them over with his dad, checking for signs of sickness, or predators, anything not being right. He and his dad kept notes on what grass the animals liked best, what they ate last and what wasn't being grazed at all. They broke off samples of grass and kept them in the coil binder with the notes. He helped whenever the cows or sheep had to be moved to a new pasture because the old one was grazed out, and he helped to isolate the ram. He and his dad were always counting. Cougars, bears, wolves and coyotes, maybe, had taken their toll on the live-stock. By the time haying was over they'd already lost eight sheep. Whether to predators or to rus-tlers wasn't certain. In the Cariboo, though, rustlers don't usually take sheep, just cattle. Eight sheep gone and only three carcasses; they were probably hauled off and eaten somewhere else.

Ten went with him everywhere, but around the animals he kept a careful distance. The cows and sheep soon got used to him. But the chickens were different. The first time Ten came up to their fence, they scurried to the opposite end of their pen and squawked in terror. Soon, though, they stopped squawking and stopped scurrying away from Ten at all. They realized he was just playing. The bolder ones stuck their heads through the wire fence and invited him to come closer. Ten approached the fence cautiously, then jumped back with a yelp when he was pecked on the nose. Chickens could play too, Jake thought. But on second thought, maybe they were just bad tempered. Eggs were sure good, though, and if cooked before they got too old the chickens were good too.

Jake's dad was happy that telling Jake when to start to work and when to stop wouldn't be necessary. Jake seemed to like doing real work, and he liked using the machinery and being left to figure things out on his own. He was gradually developing "puck sense," as his dad liked to call it, of what worked and what didn't work.

Work wasn't everything, though, and partway through August the haying was finished. After the morning chores Jake had the day to himself.

Himself and Number Ten, that is. Whenever Willy wasn't working on her own place, she was with them.

The most fun they had was hiking back to the river together. This particular river was what Jake's mom feared the most about moving to the Cariboo. The river was wildest in early summer when winter runoff was at its peak, but it was dangerous any time of year. Always fast flowing, always ice cold, always deep. Jake's parents knew and understood because they were paddlers. They had been on river trips in canoes and Mr. G. even taught canoeing. They knew from fearful experiences that a person in that water without a wet suit wouldn't have even five minutes of thinking clearly.

Fine then, but Jake still loved to go there. He didn't go swimming, of course; it was much too wild for that. What he liked to do most was sit and watch it flow by. The river was about an hour's walk west of their ranch. Mrs. G., after making Jake promise, yet again, that he wouldn't go too near the water, packed a knapsack with drinking water and food for him and Willy and Ten, and a book to read, and a sun hat and a warm sweater and his jacket, just in case it suddenly got cold or started raining or the next ice age all of a sudden was up and sitting there in his way, and he had no choice but to walk through it in order to get home. This always frightened her, but she refused to make Jake stay away, he loved that river so much. But it made her feel better knowing he had all that stuff in his pack.

Along the way Ten hunted for rabbits to chase. Rabbits always run in a circle. They run faster than coyotes, but aren't as smart. If a rabbit ran in a straight line he could outrun any coyote, but he never does. All the coyote has to do then is cut across the circle. Ten had this figured out, but all he would do is nip at the rabbit; he never killed one. He would chase and chase around and around and once he started to tire he would dash across the circle and the rabbit would practically run into him. Ten would either nip him or slow down and the rabbit would keep running in a circle. Sometimes Ten would just lie down and watch what the rabbit did next. He was a gentle soul, Number Ten.

His next favourite chase was mice, and he did this whenever there weren't any rabbits around. If he sniffed a mouse, he would paw the ground and make it scurry away under the grass like they do. Then he would chase it down and paw it and soon the mouse would have to come onto the top of the grass because there were no more tunnels to run in. Ten could catch any mouse easily, but he always made a fun chase out of it before grabbing it and tossing it into the air. He would watch it fall, let it scurry away, then pounce on it and hold it while it squealed in terror, then let go again.

Jake and Willy were lying under a big Ponderosa pine. The river passed beneath them, about ten metres down a steep cliff, and then curved wide to the west so it looked to be flowing off into the mountains. The Coast Mountains, they were called, and they were several miles from the river, across the Chilcotin Plateau. The air was hot and dry and felt sharp in their nostrils. Willy fell asleep as soon as she lay down. She always worked hard and now, at the end of haying season, she was especially tired. The Priedens had a big place and they ran eight hundred cattle. Even though there was Hal, Willy's dad, and her three older brothers, there was always plenty of work for Willy too. As soon as the last big bale was stacked near the barn, Willy's dad "ordered" her to take a week off. So she rode over to Jake's. The river was a favourite place of Willy's, too, but this particular day she was so tired she was content to lie down within sight of it. Jake heard her start to snore and turned to see a black ant crawling across the bridge of her nose. He flicked it away.

Jake was thinking that he would like to be able to smell like Ten did. Ten learned so much from smelling. There was the smell of the long-needled pine that shaded them, but little else that Jake could detect. Ten seemed to smell so much more, though.

He was drinking a juice box and eating a granola bar and watching Ten scare up mice when suddenly he was gripped with fear. What if something happened? Every night he heard rifle shots. There was the poisoned gut pile, and the rifle hanging in Griff Webster's pickup, and—the one image that Jake found hardest to shake out of his mind—the dead coyote, head shot, sprawled on the ground in their backyard.

He called Ten and made him lie down beside him. Since the day of the dead coyote he'd been tying Ten up whenever he had to go away without him. He wouldn't let him out at night, and he made sure Ten always had lots to eat, just in case he might be tempted to hunt for food. But it seemed there should be more. Jake petted Ten and hugged him and, of course, Ten didn't know what Jake was thinking. He wanted to chase mice. Finally Jake let him go. But there had to be more he could do.

For now, though, he would join Willy and have a nap. It was a hot cloudless day and Jake had been working hard, too. His muscles were sore from maneuvering bales from the wagon onto the elevator that rolled them up into the barn. He loved the feeling, though. And he could smell the pine pitch and the long thin needles that barely moved in the still August air.

Dragonflies were buzzing back and forth. He tried to follow one, but lost track as they hummed here and there so quickly. Jake knew that some birds ate dragonflies, and he marvelled that a bird could be quick enough to catch one. He felt lazy and satisfied. There was an occasional coolness in the air, lifting up from the river that was just a spit and a bit away.

He went over in his mind all that he had done in haying, making sure he remembered how to do it exactly as his dad wanted it done. He had driven the tractor for the baling and later had driven to pull the wagon, and finally had maneuvered the bales from the wagon onto the conveyer while his dad stacked them up in the barn. That was the hardest. When he was driving, he would stop beside a stook, put the tractor into neutral and wait as his dad loaded the bales and stacked them so they stayed in place as they bumped and rolled across the field. Then slide the clutch in, put it in gear and then ease out the clutch … easy and steady and …

Jake drifted off and was soon flying over the meadow. Ten was sniffing out a mouse. The ground was turning brown … it was amazing how the big stones stood out … and Jake and Willy were lying on their backs under a tree, and how curiously interesting they were. Jake loved it when he "went flying" as he called it. It was something that he had always been able to do, fly around above the trees and look down on himself. As long as he stayed just above the trees it wasn't scary, and he always got a curious thrill seeing his body down there on the ground—like something quite separate from himself.

Suddenly he heard a desperate yelp. Jake slid back into his body and snapped himself awake. He was on his feet before he remembered where he was. Ten was in trouble. He ran to the bank and scoured the river and what little he could see of the cliff face. No Number Ten in sight, but the water was fast and high. Then he heard another yelp. His heart quickened in both relief and fear. It sounded like it was coming from directly below, so he should be able to see.

"Here Ten, come on, boy," he called. Ten yipped again. Then Jake realized that he couldn't see the cliff right down to the water, but only to a few metres above where the bank suddenly went sheer. Jake raced upriver and looked back and, sure enough, there was Ten, crouched on the only grassy shelf on the cliff, looking desperate and scared. It was another five metres down to the water. The bank below Ten was steep clay, but at least it wasn't rocky.

Jake knew what he had to do. He ran to Ten's downriver side, and where the bank gradually dropped off, he went down to the water. He could just barely see Ten then, and Ten could just barely see him. He called. "Here, Ten. Come on, boy. You can do it."

Ten hesitated, then lurched to the side and hesitated again, and finally he must have figured out that there was no other way. He started down the steep bank and, sure enough, he fell over and rolled and rolled until he landed in the river. He disappeared from sight as he was immediately swept downstream. As soon as his head broke the surface, Jake called out to him.

"Ten, over here. Come on, boy. You can do it."
Ten swam furiously toward the voice, but the

current continued to pull him into the fastest water, and away from the shore. He couldn't make any progress toward Jake at all. He was swept past where Jake stood calling. Jake could see the terror in Ten's eyes. He ran along the bank to catch up, calling, "Ten, over here. You have to do this, boy. Come on. Come here. Hard. Swim hard." Ten saw Jake running even with him. Although he couldn't swim against the fast current, he was able to move toward shore by swimming across the current ever so slightly. "You have to go harder, Ten, you have to."

Jake ran along the shore, stumbling, calling out. First he stayed even with Ten, then he pulled ahead. He ran to a point and then stopped there and called desperately, "Ten, over here. Come here, boy. You have to do this. Harder now. Harder."

Jake could see Ten change gears. He sped up for a bit, then it was as though he ran out of gas. He slowed down. The current was going to take him past Jake again, too far out to reach, and Ten was slowed down already by the freezing-cold water. Jake didn't have any choice. He had to go after him.

In the river now, the water rushed by Jake's knees, then up to his thighs. He could see by the look on Ten's face that he was terrified. Jake grabbed a twisted root that was poking through the surface of the water. He yanked it hard, and it seemed solid. Using it as an anchor, he waded deeper. In up to his waist now, he knew he couldn't go in any further. The force of the current meant he could barely hang on as it was. If the root broke ... but he couldn't think about that.

"Ten! Here, Ten, come on, boy!"

Ten was swept past fast, too fast for Jake to get his arm around the coyote's neck. Stretched out as far as he could into the swirling current, Jake made a desperate grab for his tail. Got it. With one hand he pulled hard, while the other still clung to the root. Still swimming furiously, Ten swung in an arc through the water. Now, if only the root held!

But it wasn't a root after all, just a stick buried in the riverbank. The combined force of Jake, the coyote and the rushing water pulled it free. Jake yelped at the numbing cold as he was pulled off his feet. And then he had a mouthful of water as his head went under, too. Coughing and spluttering, he struggled to keep his head above water. Still holding desperately to Ten's tail, he realized that they were heading straight downstream.

He tried to call out to Ten to turn back to

shore, but he couldn't speak through the gripping cold. He tried to paddle with his free hand. Then Jake caught a glimpse of the bank speeding by and realized that Ten was indeed making progress toward that bank. Knowing instinctively that he couldn't fight the force of the river, the coyote was using the current to gradually move them closer to the shore.

Ten was doing it all by himself. Jake gripped Ten's tail with his other hand, too, and kicked his legs furiously, from the waist, not from the knees, just as he'd been taught. The only part of Ten above water was his snout. He swam with all of his strength. Finally his front paws touched the bottom and he began to claw his way frantically up the bank. Still clinging to the coyote's tail, Jake tried desperately to find the bottom with his feet. He stumbled once and almost lost his grip, but as Ten hauled himself out of the water, he pulled Jake into the shallows. On hands and knees Jake crawled out of the raging torrent.

Once free of the water's grasp, he scrambled up the bank, not stopping until he got to the top. Collapsing onto his knees he hugged a very wet and very happy Number Ten. They hugged for a long time. Ten didn't move and neither did Jake, but both their hearts were racing. So wonderful to feel the sun, to feel the cold get smaller and smaller. Water dripped onto the ground and formed a puddle between them.

Ten collapsed onto the ground. Jake let go and lay back. The sun soothed him from head to toe. He felt the tension leave, heard Ten panting beside him, and then for the first time he felt scared. He could have lost Ten forever. He saw the image over and over again, Ten floating by and him not being able to reach. His entire body shook at the thought of what could have happened.

He just lay there in the sun and gradually his breathing became normal. He thought about the cold water and what it did to him, how it held him in its grip and wouldn't allow him to breathe, to move, even to think. How his forehead hurt the most, how everything seemed to just stop working as he floated madly along.

He sat up and looked down at the river. The fear came back. A wild, uncontrollable fear that made him want to run away. Jake couldn't leave this way. He wouldn't. He slid down the bank and squatted at the water's edge. Holding his hand in the cold water, he watched the river rush by. He stayed that way until the fear passed. Jake Grant loved that river. He refused to let it make him afraid.

On his way back up the bank, he watched Ten shake. The water came off his fur in tiny drips that the sun shone through like crystals, so Ten was encircled in a thousand tiny glistenings of silver-white light.

Jake sat down again. He petted Ten and he hugged him. Dumb as it sounded, he felt that someone else had been there helping him do the rescue and keeping him safe. Not a real person, of course. There weren't any other people around except Willy, and she was asleep. But someone else had been there nonetheless.

Side by side, Jake and Ten walked back to where Willy lay under the tree.

"Hey, Will, let's go home."

"What?"

"How be we go home now?"

"Okay," Willy muttered.

"I'll take the pack," Jake said, stuffing things back inside.

As they began their walk home, Ten stepped along beside Jake and was quiet. It was almost as though he, too, was thinking it all over carefully.

Willy was just waking up. "You guys go swimmin' or somethin'?"

"Yeah," was all Jake said.

"Your mom will kill you. That's not a swimmin'

river, you know."

"Yeah, I know." They were walking side by side.

"I don't even go swimming in the river. Too fast. Too cold."

"It wasn't intentional," Jake said.

"Oh. You fell in?"

"Ten fell in. I had to go after him."

"Oh-oh … Your mom isn't going to like this."

"Yeah." Jake didn't feel like talking anymore. They walked the rest of the way without saying anything. When they got to the yard, Willy got on her bike and headed for home.

Jake walked into the kitchen with Number Ten close beside him. Mrs. G. knew immediately that something had gone wrong. They were still wet, of course, but that wasn't it. It was something else, something to do with being a mother.

"Hi."

"What on earth … " She lifted the pack off his back and looked all over him, checking for blood-stains. When she didn't find any she was relieved, but just a bit relieved.

"Ten fell in the river."

"And you?"

"I had to get him."

"You went in after him?"

"I had to."

"Jacob!" Her voice rose until she was almost screaming. "You could have drowned. The river is too fast and too cold. You should never be near it!"

Her mother's tone frightened him more than the river had. "I can swim. I'm fine. Ten's fine."

She felt the beginnings of losing control, then she steeled herself. "Come with me."

Taking her eldest child by the wrist, she led him to the upstairs bathroom. She put the drain plug in place and turned on the hot water full blast. Then she turned to Jake and stripped off his clothes. He didn't like being naked in front of his mother, but knew that complaining when she was in this state of mind was pointless. He endured her rubbing his body down with the towel.

Mrs. G. checked the water temperature, then mixed in some cold. Then she went back to rubbing him down. She had to touch him, to be sure he was alright.

"Okay, Mom." She was rubbing so hard that it hurt.

She checked the water again. "It's ready now." She was being intense, almost fierce. She directed him into the tub and he sat down. "As hot as you can stand it. I'll be right back."

His mom left for downstairs and Jake was a tad disappointed that she was gone. The hot water *did* feel good. And the rubdown had felt terrific, if only a bit hard. He realized that he had been holding everything back. Had he felt scared? Not really. Only when he first realized Ten was in serious trouble. After that he was too busy. Cold? Not until it was over. He started to feel cold partway home. What was Ten like after being pulled out of the river? He was happy and quiet.

Jake called, "Ten! Here, boy," and his mom answered.

"I just gave him hot milk. I'll bring him up in a minute."

Hot milk for Number Ten. Jake started to cry. He cried until he heard his mom on the stairs and then he stopped. He wetted his face with water so she couldn't tell.

She carried a mug of hot chocolate and a plate of cookies. Ten was right behind her.

"Careful, it's hot."

Jake slurped some down. Then he popped a whole peanut butter cookie into his mouth. His mom, watching him, broke down. She had seen him pop a whole cookie into his mouth so many times before, he must be all right. She threw her arms around him and hugged and hugged. He felt confused at first, but then he thought he understood and squeezed her back.

"Alright, Mom," Jake said. He was focusing on the hot chocolate, trying not to spill any.

She let go. "It's okay. I'm okay now. Oh, Jake …" Then she hugged him again and this time hot chocolate *did* spill into the bathwater, and they both laughed.

Being in the river with Number Ten became one of those things that was bigger to look back on than it had been when it happened. Gradually Jake realized that something terrible could have happened. But more frightening than that, he had come closer to losing Ten than ever before. It sure made him think.

Chapter 14
The Red Bandanna

Jake and Ten were on the sofa watching television. Since getting out of the river, they had barely left each other's side. It was around nine, and Jake was so tired he was thinking he might go to bed. Mrs. G. had been waiting on him since she ran his bath several hours ago. She was still fearful of the tale he had told. She held this fear inside her that he could up and disappear forever unless she kept him in sight.

Jake didn't hear the black pickup drive fast into the yard and skid to a stop in front of the kitchen window. Moving quickly, Griff Webster got out and lowered the tailgate. Then he pulled on a piece of plastic, sliding both it and its contents onto the ground. On the plastic was the mangled carcass of a calf. More like a skeleton, really, as almost all of the flesh had been torn away. It was a fresh kill; there were no maggots or bugs yet, and the crows and ravens had not yet pecked out the eyes. When Griff had first come upon the carcass an hour earlier, there had been just a trace of warmth when he touched the calf's head. He took a last look, shook his head in sorrow, then got back into the truck and peeled angrily out the lane.

Jake didn't hear him arrive, but he heard him drive away. He got up and looked out the window and then rushed outside. Seeing the dead calf was not as much of a shock as seeing the dead coyote had been. But Jake felt sick just the same, only this time he made himself all tight inside and then looked over the mangled carcass. It was not a pretty sight. He touched the guts to see if they were warm. Barely. No single animal could have done that much damage so quickly, he reasoned. Jake heard the door open behind him and shortly his father stood at his side.

"Damn him," Mr. G. said. "I've had just about enough of this."

"What can we do?"

"You just watch me." Jake's dad moved toward his truck.

"Wait!" Jake said. He could see his dad's temper building again and this frightened him. "Let us do it. Ten and me."

"And just what do you and Ten have in mind?"

"Talk to him. I've got this feeling, Dad. I think he might listen to me." Jake was remembering that sad, lonely look on his neighbour's face the day he and Willy were racing. How the first time they met, Griff Webster looked at him as though he knew him from someplace.

"From what I've seen, that man doesn't listen to anybody."

"Could I try? Please?"

"Alright. I'll give you this one chance, and if that doesn't work, we do it my way. But not now. It's late and everybody's tired. First thing in the morning you can go over on your bike. Besides, Griff's a drinker. I'd feel a whole lot better if he was sober when you talk to him."

"Okay," Jake said. "Right after breakfast then."

For the second time in recent weeks, Mr. G. loaded the remains of a dead animal into the front-end loader of the Massey. He again tossed shovel in the bucket with the carcass and headed for the bush, the tractor lights creating a bubble of light that crept through the night. Mr. G. drove slowly. He wanted time to think.

Jake went back inside. He said goodnight to his mom, tolerating another one of her hugs. Then he and Ten went up to his room. He got into his peejays and then lay with his head at the foot of his bed and looked out the window. Tomorrow morning, then ... he had some thinking to do.

When he woke up it was light out and he was still at the foot of the bed. His mom must have come in during the night and covered him up. He remembered lying that way so he could think, but that was all he remembered. He must have fallen asleep right away. No matter. This thing that he had to do didn't have to be planned in every detail. Jake knew in his gut what had to happen. The words would be there when he needed them.

He ate breakfast and then got ready. He put Ten's collar on and then got some bailer twine for a leash. He got his bike from the shed and attached the leash to Ten's collar and rode out the lane. Ten had been on a leash only once before. For him it was some kind of game.

But for Jake things could not have been more serious. He was using the leash out of his fear that if Griff Webster saw the coyote running free he just might shoot. This thought drove him on. There was also the image of the dead coyote that wouldn't leave his mind, and now the dead calf was there, too. As he got closer to his neighbour's lane, his stomach became more tense and his mind became more focused. What he was doing had to be done. There was no other way. But if someone had asked him what he was going to say, he would not have been able to answer. At the same time he knew what he was going to say. For Jake it was one of those complicated inside things that he couldn't explain to anyone, much less to himself.

He turned into the lane at the Webster ranch, and there was Griff working on his hay rake. He was changing a belt. It was a lot of work for something so simple. Griff was in a worse mood than normal because of this. He was so used to the morning-after effects of drinking that he didn't feel hung over at all.

Whenever Jake saw him, he felt tiny beside his neighbour's bulk. Griff wore coveralls over his green work clothes. The coveralls were grease stained and had lots of holes, and it all made the man even scarier.

Jake stopped his bike about ten metres away. Griff had seen him ride in and had continued working as though there was nothing unusual going on. Jake laid his bike down and tied Ten to the crossbar. Ten seemed to have figured out that something big was going on. He sat quietly, but paid close attention.

"Morning, sir."

Griff looked intently at Jake, then he seemed to remember something and looked quickly away.

"I'm Jake Grant, your neighbour."

"I know."

"Could I talk to you?"

"I guess."

"My dad and I changed the belt on our rake, too."

No reply.

"Ours wasn't broken, though. It was just worn through. Dad thought it might break."

"That right."

"Bad time for a breakdown. But then, it always seems to happen at the worst time."

"That's so."

"Dad and I just finished a few days ago with the haying."

"Yup."

"I drove the tractor. First time."

"That so."

"I'll be doing tractor work from now on, I guess."

"How old?"

"Eleven."

"Name? Jake, is it, or Jacob?"

"Jacob, really, but everybody calls me Jake."

"That a fact."

Griff was thinking of his eldest grandchild. Martin was his name. Everyone called him Marty. He was just a year younger than Jake.

"Ah, sir?"

"What?"

"I'm afraid you're going to shoot Ten."

"You mean that?" He tossed his head toward the bike.

"Yes, sir. That's my dog."

"That ain't no dog."

"Not exactly, maybe."

"That ain't no dog."

"He's been in the house all night."

"Small mercy, that."

"Sir?" Jake waited a long moment, and then finally Griff Webster said,

"What?"

"I love him. Number Ten. That's what I wanted to say."

"You rode over here to tell me that?"

"Yes, sir."

Jake watched tears welling up in Griff Webster's eyes. Then the big man turned away. His chest heaved and then heaved again. Jake stepped toward him and put his hand on Griff's arm. His chest heaved another time, and then another and another. Jake squeezed what he could of the big arm, and the adjustable wrench slid out of Griff's hand and with his arms hanging straight down at his sides Griff cried and cried.

Jake didn't feel uncomfortable as he watched his big neighbour cry. He thought of himself in the bathtub the day before. And he knew that if something happened to Ten he would cry again for sure.

"There is one more thing," he said at last.

"What?" Griff mumbled.

"I wanted to say I was sorry to hear about Trixie and your wife."

About half an hour later Griff Webster's black pickup turned slowly into the Grants' laneway, eased down to the yard and then came to a stop in front of the kitchen window. Jake's bike was in the back. Jake was in the passenger seat. Ten sat in the middle between him and Griff. Around Ten's neck there was a red bandanna. While Elsa watched from inside, both Mr. and Mrs. G. came out to see what was up.

Griff smiled, and this alone almost stopped Jake's parents in their tracks. They saw Jake, of course, and he was smiling, and they saw Number

Ten sitting in the middle with an intelligent look on his face and that red bandanna around his neck. Understandably, Mr. and Mrs. G. were confused.

Griff laughed. Then, indicating Ten, he said, "Looks pretty good, don't he?"

Mrs. G. recovered first. "I think he looks great," she said.

"Figured I better do somethin' to set this one apart from all them other ones. You know," Griff added, "so's he doesn't get himself shot by some irate rancher."

There was an awkward moment that ended when Mrs. G. said, "Well, that's great. And he looks so good in red."

"What's more," Griff said, "this fine boy of yours tells me that Number Ten is partial to ice cream. I figure that works out just fine. I happen to have a particular fondness for a DQ milkshake. So I thought I might take these two into town an' buy 'em a treat. That be okay with you?"

Now Mr. G. had recovered enough to speak. "That would be fine." He was still uncertain, though. You could tell by his voice. So Mrs. G. said, "That's a great idea. Have a good time."

"Back in an hour or so," Griff said.

He turned his truck around and eased out the lane.

Jake leaned out the window and waved good-bye. He was feeling good. The only thing weighing on his mind now was whether to have a strawberry or a chocolate milkshake.